Memo on Trans-Atlantic Flight 6006, Destination Paris

Clues are few enough in any plane crash. In this case the flight recorder is also missing. But seven miles from the left wing we found a suede traveling purse. Inside, most of the photos, love letters and telephone tapes survived undamaged. Our investigating team at first dismissed these, as too personal to relate to the twisted facts of destruction. But, after transcribing and translating, we realized differently. The purse is our black box! It tells a disturbing story, however appealing. If death is a great denier, so is love. We're still looking for a bomb, but evidence is equivocal. It's not certain that the writers of the letters were among the passengers. Their names aren't on the manifest, but two victims aren't identified yet. Was one on the ground? Was he the target? Was she carrying explosives? Answers are uncertain. Nevertheless, as close as this couple came to be, they hardly knew each other. Her innocence is sly, his humor revealing. Obsession and opportunity inspired their romance. Are they playing with us from the grave? Are we their death grin? Or was their love after all impossible? Did they disappear themselves deliberately? Are we being short-sighted? Is the joke on us? We've yet to locate anyone, who will help us to a conclusion. Perhaps the phone tapes and the long-distance letters speak clearly enough. We need your opinion. Please report immediately.

Nancy Dawson Stiles and Elihu Le Blot,
Investigating agents

May 23, 1992

on the crest of time

a historical romance
circa 1990

XY Zebra

firefall^{tm}

First Edition: October 1998

Printed in the United States of America

ISBN: 0-915090-14-7
Library of Congress: 96-083139

Lithography: McNaughton & Gunn
Design: Apple/Adobe/Quark

FIREFALL EDITIONS
Canyon California 94516-0189

firefallmedia@worldnet.att.net

My Dear Mr. Optic,

Suddenly your bamboo blinds insist on privacy. Worse, they hide your camera display. The cherrywood Deardorf on the brick window shelf drew me into your shop in the first place. It created a sense of age, authority and trust that is no longer visible. I hope the earthquake didn't damage your treasures too much. Nonetheless I have another problem for you. The Gundlach you sold me isn't genuine. It's also broken. These faults didn't cause the quake, nor were they a consequence. Could I have kept to my schedule I would be in Europe now, alone with my disappointment. As I'm still here, I expect you to act correctly, and see to my complaint. Do you always take advantage of women this way?

    I made a special trip to San Francisco today, to find you. You must know that, with the bridge collapsed, getting this far was both tedious and a trial. The kind owner of the Litteraria has lent me paper and pen. (I'm in her shop now, across the cable car street.) I do hope you have not concealed yourself permanently, and that power and service will be restored soon, to Russian Hill.

    My office, lab and home phone numbers are listed below. (I was untouched.) Are you ever in the East Bay?

Sincerely,
Sara Berlin

23 October 1989

Dear Sara —

What luck! You're dissatisfied, you've come back. The store's a
shambles, my flat's flattened, and I couldn't be happier. I never
expected to see you again.

I don't grasp the problem though. I explained. You understood. I sell only originals, but of my own making. Definitely!
My brochure goes into detail. Each camera does one thing well,
especially the mock German models. The camera you bought
was a *LACH*, a "Laugh!" And it works. I tested it myself, but
it focuses like most Germans, 10" in front of its nose and 10"
inside its nose. All other distances are as blurry as optical
physics. I.e., it's an excellent close-up camera, it magnifies
like a microscope. It's useful and useless at once.

If you want a true Gundlach, I have a vintage model from
the Thirties, but it doesn't look German at all. The black
bubble levels, the endless knurled knobs, the overly engineered
intricacies are entirely missing. Indeed it's built like a simple
piece of fine mahogany furniture. You won't find a saw burn
or overcut anywhere, even inside. It has green leather bellows.
And it's twice the price.

Would you like to go to dinner? La Petite Cafe, down the
block, has a new menu. Satisfaction guaranteed.

Tschüss,
André Optic

Dear André,

I must be losing it. I did lose it that day in your shop. You entranced and intimidated me with your familiarity of photography. I felt very uncomfortable not having your understanding, but you put me at ease, so I bought what I thought you were inviting me to buy. It was the deeply knowing smile in your dark eyes that seduced me, as if they saw more than the cameras could.

This is silly. Yes, yes, you interest me also, but it's near impossible to start anything now. My departure is immanent.

All right, I will go to dinner with you, but only if you explain yourself first.

I took apart the camera to discover that you silvered the rim edge, of the lens elements, so that I would see my own eyes enlarged as well, unless I was wholly centered.

Were you laughing at me too, when you sold me the camera? I am Austrian, not German. Can you tell the two apart? Or do you share the usual American prejudices against my better country?

Yes, Yes, I am also a scientist, an astro-chemist who works on the sub-molecular level. But you could not know that. My research into rare metals as produced by stars is finished here (along with my doctorate). But I didn't reveal to you my background, or my future plans, to extend my micro-analysis to isotopes, in Europe. Are you just a good guesser?

Send me the real Gundlach, on approval, and if it works for me, I will pay both for dinner and your price accordingly.

Yours,
Sara Berlin

Dear André,

The antique camera arrived by special messenger. Thank you for your trust. The absence of a note from you, or apology, disappointed me though.

Unfortunately I am going to disappoint you also. I tested both cameras, against each other, very thoroughly.

Yes, yes, the "Laugh!" does work perfectly at a fixed distance, and the magnification is truly macroscopic, but not to the probing power I need.

The Gundlach may be authentic, but it's inadequate also. It isn't broken in the normal sense, but something is wrong with the pictures. I would buy it as a vintage camera because it has the look of a certain time, but it does not photograph that way. The pictures are crisp and hard with contrast. They seem so present. The haze of time is missing. Maybe I am in the wrong country. Everything here is meant to be new, or disguised to be, and can not help being what it is. I am not anti-American, but I know of what I speak, as I have been here seven years. (Sometimes I feel like Josepha in Egypt — are you acquainted with the feminist version of the bible?)

Where did you learn German anyway? You look Slavic.

Do you still want to take me to dinner? Tell me also, what do you think of feminism? Contrary to media opinion, it is not dead!

(I have tried to call but your phone is still traumatized.)

Happy Equinox,
Sara Berlin

Imagine if my cameras were all ideal, you'd simply be gone.

Nothing will satisfy you though. Your vision's fixed and broken at once. Your earthquake's inside. Definitely! Are you always this difficult?

Don't you realize? My camera is the picture! The way it looks is the way you should see. Whether a model works or not is irrelevant, though each camera will flexibly and well. You only have to assert your mastery. I've already tested the limits.

So — surprise, surprise — you're an astro-chemist, neither chemist or astronomer but a hybrid, of your own design.

My cameras are too, you see. Even the "Laugh!" is a cross between an oscilloscope reader and a microscope. Essentially there's nothing new under the sun, only our rediscovery of it. Why we're doomed to re-invent the world ever and again is a problem I enjoy struggling with. There appears no escape. Every star's beyond reach. In essence every camera's already built. Even every starlet's been dreamed. What do you see in molecular spectra? Are you only a data analyst? Is the camera you want after all a computer, a blind keyboard and a pixel screen?

Whatever you sense of my excitements, you haven't talked me out of taking you to dinner, so the invitation stands. And now to try I'll answer your questions.

Feminism? Can't say I think much of it at all. My cameras do what I tell them to.

Speak German, me? No, but I've a dictionary that does. My father learned reluctantly — he was 7 years old in World War One — when his village in Russia was overrun. Retreating Imperial soldiers burned his family home. The advancing Teutonic army redug his basement as the most-forward trench

on the front line and shipped him and his 5 brothers to
Prussian schools in the rear. Ever since, even in defeat, lager
Germs have claimed the area, but the locals grow up now with
nuclear guns and load them facing west. They have to, because
the German AAA map defines my father's Russian homeland as
"administered territory" even now. Oh yes, with my mom, my
dad used the little he remembered, to keep me from understanding, when I was 7.

Make fun of you? No, I wanted you to laugh at yourself.
You managed a sneer. You went directly to the most complex
instrument and stared at it with such serious sadness, you gave
your longing away. I didn't choose the camera, you did. I also
recognized your softer accent, subtle though it is, from old war
movies. But I knew nothing about you, and didn't need to
guess. I didn't have to. I watched your changes.

By chance, if you still want an original antique to mist out
the world for you, you'll need a lens at least 100 years old. I've
one in a 6" brass mount, with an aperture wheel, made in Paris
in the last century.

Should I bring it to dinner? You're invited back to my shop
after dessert also. Definitely!

If my phone's working tomorrow — I've been promised by
an anonymous voice that it will be — I'll call. I'm here round
the clock now, living in the back. My apartment in the Marina
was bulldozed. The police gave me an hour to get out what I
could reach.

By the way, do you have any rare heavy metals sitting at
home, that you can spare? Maybe we can formula something
new into being.

Expectantly,
André

 20.10.89   9:30:02

"You have reached Sara Berlin in her newest orbit. I am outside the capsule. Should you wish to proceed, wait for the signal. Automatic telemetry will beam your message to me. Beeeeep!"

"Hello Sara. André here, from my own phone. How about tonight? *Seelachs* is the menu. I made special reservations. The fish are waiting to be eaten. Come whenever, and stay. A weekend in San Francisco's ahead, if you'd like. I've room here and in my life for you."

   *"André answering service. Definitely! Zzrreeeeeeep!"*

"André, your machine is illiterate or hysteric, which? Or is there a rude side to you I have yet to see? Yes, yes, this is Sara, at twelve noon. I will arrive at eight, somehow, perhaps by ferry. Are you always so bold? I hope not, but flirt as you will, I expect a refund. Or better yet, can you make your cameras right for me?"

 20.10.89   15:27:00

"You have reached Sara Berlin in parabolic orbit. Please leave a message in the electronic wind to guide me. Beeeeep!"

"Hi Sara, bring extra clothes, the way you'd like to look, a hundred years ago. I've a new lens ready. *Chooᵧze."*

Dear André,

I am embarrassed. Should I be? What must you think of me
now? Did the pictures work out? I am very anxious to see them.
No one ever wanted to photograph me before so intimately. I
must admit, I wanted you to do everything you did, from the
moment I walked into your shop and saw the nude on the wall,
of the appealingly awkward woman with a long face and short
nose. She might be my sister if I had one. I wondered right then
if I would let you photograph me revealingly and how I might
appear. Now I will know what you really think of me, and if
you are as good, as you must suppose you are. Regardless it was
fun — But tell me what you think, I know what I think. Truly I
am hesitant to face you, and see myself. Tell me, how do I look?
As you expected? Are you excited still? Tell my machine. It will
tell me.

Thank you for the wonderful weekend. I had a lovely time,
even though we did not go out again after dinner. I have
already forgotten what the food was like. I kept waiting for you
to reach out and touch me, and when you did, I wanted you to
hold me forever. But you know that I am leaving. I must buy
my ticket today.

Thank you also for changing the lens on the *"Lach"*.
Europe will never look the same to me, I hope. I am not
sure what I learned however. You did not give me a chance
at the film plane. You took over the controls completely.

Incidentally, I have a platinum thermometer. Where do
you want it?

And, my parents used English as their secret language at
home, to keep things from me, when I was young. That is why
I learned so well.

With love, Sara

Dear Sara,

The pictures are perfect! The negatives seem 100 years old.
When I bring out their qualities in the printing, you'll be
delighted. You'll see yourself in the chemical light of another
era. The brass lens simply obeyed its own optics. But you at
3 a.m. — stripping under the street-lamp was so daring and
unexpected. The fog on the hill also did for you what the reality
of time can't. In almost every image you mist into yourself
darkly. The glow of the fog doesn't penetrate far. A deeply
shadowed purpose holds you. In turn you embrace the shy
secrets of time. You do. Definitely.

It was the same on earthquake night. The damage to
Russian Hill was small and mainly to the power supplies.
Everything was dark and cold and quiet. The cable car ran
without lights. A truck went slowly ahead to warn of its
coming. The persistence of the machine in its track under
pre-arranged power was eerie. The image is etched in me. I'd
a curious sense of fear and fatal surprise, as I do now with you.

Indeed I was in the darkroom in the back of my shop, when
the earthquake rocked the trays empty and brought my shelves
down. I heard the building crack and crawled out sure that I'd
be hit on the way by the ceiling falling. Instead you happened.
Your letter is the next thing I remember. It's strange and
special, having you as my aftershock.

In actual fact, the earthquake's uprooted most of my
neighbors and friends. Change is in the air. Even where it was
not, the earthquake's an excuse for it to be. When the tremors
started, I thought, this is a good one. They kept on annoyingly,
the exposure was wasted, the paper in the enlarger ruined.

Suddenly the shock waves slapped me sideways. Panicked, my heart raced, at the nearing crush of death. I feel similarly about you. The photos reveal you. They surprised me. You seem so fragile, as if you'd wither and vanish, with the street lamp facing you directly. This is just a darkroom impression, but still —

It's cold and lonely now, living in the shop. Definitely, but the sunset's consoling. A glowing jet trail, slicing the burning clouds, lifts me out of here. I thought the earthquake was my chance to move to the woods, even those across the bay, but here I still am for now.

I called all your numbers but only your tape was reachable. The mail seems the quickest way across the bay these days. I hear the subway opens again next week, though it'll still close at midnight, and that the base of the San Mateo bridge moved 11" permanently. Engineers jacked it up, with traffic running, and returned it to within a foot of its usual path.

But then too, you said originally you'd be gone in 2 days, and it's now been a week. Enclosed are 3 contact sheets. Pick what you want me to print, an image from each perhaps.

When can I see you again? I would've read this into your space-age machine, but not without knowing who else might hear.

love,
André

Dear André,

Danke! Danke! Thank you, thank you!
Really I look pretty good. You can not see me clearly in
your pictures. Honestly I'm impressed. You are a visionary.
I do not see anything of what you do. Will you still guide me?
My life is not like yours, fortunately, but I need a *guter Rat.*
Normally my routine is dull and boring beyond measure.
There are no earthquakes in it. My lights did not go out.
My phone still rang. I barely felt the shaking. Nothing of it
interfered with my calendar. Can you discipline me, to see
the way you do?
I bought my ticket at last. I leave in two weeks. Yes, yes,
even though you are the excitement of my life. You have re-
awakened things in me that I thought long dead. But how can I
dream of happiness again, when it seems a hundred years ago?
In the century past — I might have been fragile, or
Madame Curie. I have always felt capable though. Here and
now the competition at the *Uni* is so intense, that even the
brightest feel stupid. Still I have reassembled your "Laugh!" so
well, you will not find a nick on the screwheads. So, am I just
another score on yours?
The last photographs of myself that I liked were made when
I was twelve, before I became a woman. I visited my grandmother in her garden then. There is much wasted green space
in Vienna, especially in the center of the city.
Why do you not come with me to Europe? There would be
enough money for both of us, if we live like students. How old
are you anyway? I am twenty-seven and three months, and I
have savings, even if you do not. I have a fellowship waiting,
in any case, in West Germany.

You must visit the places you make fun of, yes? Your ammunition will be more accurate. Besides, there is more to criticize than you can imagine. And, it will be good to see you as the foreigner.

Meanwhile, we have to talk about birth control. You have a very bad attitude. Bluffing does not work in the game of baby poker. Your remark about wearing rubbers, being the same as taking a shower with a raincoat on, was not appreciated. And I do not have to explain why. I have never been pregnant, nor do I plan to be, though in principle I am not against children at some future indefinite time.

Come visit me. See what my life is like. I do not work in an observatory. I work in the basement at the university. My experiments are attached to a computer that sees for me, that is true, but I am an experimentalist. Now I study one molecule at a time in a vacuum chamber and nano-pulse each in turn with lasers of differing wave lengths — all invisible as they are ultra-violet.

No one else hears my messages.

Are you married secretly?

Would you marry me?

Lovingly,
Sara

Dear Sara,

What a wonderful weekend! You're even better in your own
bed. Or were you inspired by the strangely decorative way in
which you live, with your carpets the same gray-blue as your
Astro-Physical journals?

Am I the padding to your split-personality? Never buy a
one-sided rug, my father used to say, after his college days
in France.

He also liked to say, Austrians are constipated Germans,
even at home, in the gilt tomb of Vienna. He said so often.
Definitely! Was he half-right or half-wrong?

Seriously, I can't say myself, that I was overawed with our
lab visit, or by what you call serious science. You and your
colleagues looked like victims of your own experiments, with
laser burns in your hands and your noses dripping constantly.
The lab is unhealthy, with its high levels of low-frequency
radiation. What are you doing to yourself? Or is that part of
another experiment, to see how alien an environment you can
live in? Will you go strange on me? How weird can you get?

Your half-sized colleague Nili cornered me at length about
photo-dissociation. The idea intrigues me. Does it only mean
laser blasting? "Your cameras are just as complex, only lower
voltage," she said.

And what's with Anemone Angst? She with the crawly hair
who climbed into the vacuum chamber and refused to come
out. Trudbert and Walburt, the visiting Prussian post-doc
twins, struck me as lunatics also. They kept talking about
magnetically tunable cavities and your cousin Odo. What
kind of name is that?

The earthquake geologist was a kick though, the one
who fell into the lab shouting, "I found the epicenter!"

However, what impressed me most about the weekend
was your remark, "The only thing definite is that I'm leaving."

Will you? Must you? The words still echo through me.

Oh yes, I am older than you, by 4 years, but you're taller
than me, by a fraction, even though you slouch to hide it,
so we're even.

I've been rereading your letters. Is it really too late for us?
Here is the lab picture, the only one you allowed.

Photographing, I expose myself, as well as the film.

There's an unseen life in you I long to bring out.

Don't let events decide our future for us. Definitely.

We can travel in detours, to give ourselves a new past
and invent a bridge of ten thousand tomorrows. Yeah!

The sky is on fire tonight. Sunset over the Pacific is always
beautiful. Still, it turns me around, toward the light in you.
It's what we share.

With love,
André

Dear André —

Oh, please do not sulk and stay away. Love me as long as I'm here. I am having a good-bye party. Everyone not in the lab when you were is curious about you. You are the first real man that I have introduced there.

Scientists are no exception. They love gossip too.

Also, as you may have guessed, the future is optical not magnetic. Light not touch reveals the world. Your improvisational ability with lens and camera construction may help us all. Anemone said as much also.

She is my favorite friend this year. She met her husband at a tennis weekend. That is as fine a place as any. He picked her racket. She kept his balls. That is as good as selling me a broken camera and then making it right, and me as well.

The party will be boring, but the people won't. Odo would be there, but he is in Germany now remeasuring the volt. Nili is the Keeper of the *Uni* Computer. She writes poems in computer too, like "nasty square wave, measured in cities, interdigitation, star dot star" and "fast bus, slow dos, brutal reboot, global undo" or "press enter to exit help", a found line. Computer haiku, she calls it. She used to write radar poetry, surface blips that hint of a real world somewhere else.

I told her that you said you would marry me, at least in theory. Did you mean that? If so, I will be back in a year, after I finish my next stage of research, I promise. There is no one else, only my ideal of Madame Curie, and my cave-loving father.

I would stay now if I had an elegant excuse, like an offer of tenure at Stanford, or at least an instructorship. What can you arrange, Mr. Salesman?

Whatever, I am writing to express my commitment to you, so that it is forever before you.

Also, I thanked you in my thesis. Your name is on the acknowledgement page after Los Alamos, who supplied the hydrogen isotopes, and the Department of Defense, who supplied the money. I was not sure what to be thanking you for, but I am so thankful for you.

What impressed me most about our last weekend was that you remembered my shopping list when I forgot it — the baker's cheese, the celery root, everything on it, completely. None of the people in my lab would have. I have never met anyone like you. Have you been trained? By whom?

I hope it is not too late for us. Why did you not find me sooner? You argue so well with your tongue. I thought I would never love again like that. Nili was jealous. She is into conjugation.

Be well, my love,
Sara

p.s.   I showed Nili the photographs.
       The way he froze the light is exquisite, she said.
       He can leaf-print me to his page, Anemone said.
       No, you may not!

Dear André,

The party is Saturday night. Come Friday. Bring a camera.
Teach me to use mine.

I am in the final days of my thesis, even though I have
graduated. The thesis is not filed yet, but it is approved. I just
have to perfect the language, so that each chapter is acceptable
as a journal article. Can you help? My computer is acting up. It
is very difficult for me right now. I spend all day and night at
my terminal. I see numbers spinning on the screen in my sleep;
it is like a slot machine without a jackpot. I dream female
symbols racing in rows, under the message, 'print this screen
and send it'. Suddenly the computer goes into a state of total
amnesia, and I wake up.

There are nine Nobel scientists here at the university. One
day I hope to have my picture on the wall too.

But there is an irreversibility stage in the impressionistic
cycle, in the eye, and it continually directs me back to you,
over and over again.

I must get ready to travel now, though my spirit will hold
you forever.

I love you,
Sara

Dear Sara,

When're you coming back? I watched the plane slant into the sky and wanted to fly after you without wings. I'm glad we're not angels though. Your eyes wouldn't be as large and sad and knowing, or your hair hennaed so brightly. Your lips might be as purple, but your breasts wouldn't cup in my hands as well. Definitely! If anyone asks, are we innocent or offending in our appetites, the answer is both. Cupid's still lustful across the Atlantic, but newborn as a baby here, sometimes.

I hate to admit, in your party dress-up I barely recognized you. You're beyond me really. That you're a molecule inspector, basically living underground, trying to graph the invisible, is very strange. What dark pleasure, what energy of calculation, is hidden inside you, in spite of your love of gauzy colors? I have to admit, the more appealing your clothes, the quicker I want to tear them off.

After your plane left, I went straight back to the shop and slept all day, on my hard bed in the back. The room seemed empty, uninhabited even by me, when I woke.

I was tempted to visit your lab, your laser-mazed halls, just to feel your presence. Even though you've cleared out your office completely and ended your experiments, you're still there, in the sense that only you fully understand the place. The long endless corridors, the layered overhead pipes, the locked libraries, the warning lights, the emergency showers, must be much like the paths in your mind.

In contrast, the party was fun. It was also curious that every foreign student I met considered himself an expert and advisor on immigration first.

The East Indian national, with his round brown face and proper English manners, best expressed the common sentiment, when he said, "We have to thank our great mother the university for our presence here, at whose bosom we all feed. May she long continue!"

Yet you've left and couldn't wait to leave, and your country imposes a two year home requirement before you can return.

Will you come back, still the prospector without a tan, wearing tennis shoes, with a 900 key chained to you, like the other molecule hunters I met?

If you've rediscovered love in yourself here, Germany's the wrong place to have it weighed or assayed. Germany is a graveyard by every measure. Three of my uncles became ashes there.

The life shadowed in you still intrigues me. Come what may, you've taken my heart with you too. But I must take care of myself. Definitely!

Last night I dreamed of trying to kill a machinist, who was stripping my cameras. He was hollow and mindless and just wouldn't die. My knife couldn't cut his tungsten-rubber eyes. I woke, my mouth full of blood, clumped, unable to clot. I should see a dentist. Don't worry. This isn't usual. The dream had a sense of ritual, of necessity, but it's the first ever I've dreamed of myself as a killer. I'm not at all. Just frustrated, more than I ever imagined I'd be, and lacking fresh fruit and vegetables. I eat out too much now.

Life is very strange, isn't it?

Your lover,
André

"André! Is it you? *Fantastisch!* There is love in your voice. So much. My mother is whining at me and criticizing, that I am thinner than ever. She says I left with such nice breasts. Should I show her your pictures of me?"

"Will I have to photograph her too?"

"God prevent! She picked me up at Schwechat — Vienna's airport, it is next to a state refinery but cozy — she takes me back tomorrow. I am leaving for Germany. My cousin rented a studio for me, large, skylit, big enough for both of us, if you come."

"I would, but I'm trying not to be jealous."

"I think about you all the time."

"Someone else'll break into your thoughts. A year'll make us strangers again. I'm afraid —"

"There is only you."

"What if you're flirted with?"

"I won't respond."

"And if you're lonely?"

"I'll write to you."

"And if you can't sleep?"

"I'll count sheep."

"And if all three happen at once?"

"I'll cry, but right now I am recording our conversation."

"Oh, that's the static! The machine's taping itself. Switch it off...."

"Tell me first, are you ready to turn over your life to me?"

"Hardly. What star are you watching?"

Dear André,

It is great to hear you on the phone, but I would much rather ferry across the bay to you, to share a plate of salmon in a small cafe, or relax in contortions on your bed, or pose for you naked under a streetlight, or sleep in your arms while you talk about the other love in your life (lenses), or introduce you at a party, or show you my molecule collection or let you criticize me or — just to be with you.

André my love, I miss you so much.
Sara

Dear Sara,

My dreams are soothing again. I stare at your pictures till I'm hypnotized. Let the grain become skin, the silver lighten softly, the dream live, let me be with you always. Definitely! My love runs quick for you now, my heart ticks toward you. I long to revisit your forgotten childhood gardens. I was an only child too.

Soon my love, and always,
André

Dearest André,

Winter will be dark and cheerless without you. Life is a bleak experiment here. Tell me what I can look forward to, when we meet again.

My lab is above ground now, I wish it were not. Northern Germany is so damp and dreary. All day it grows gradually grayer. When there is sun it sets dimly. It never rises above the rows of matchstick trees. The rain rots everything. It is cold without snow, soggy without growth, and the people also are rude and boring.

They speak a strange German here, a throat clearing, stuffed-nose cough. It requires 25% more paper, when written.

I should not have come. It was a mistake! Today for two minutes the sun found my window. Letting the rays in ruined my experiment. I do not care. It is so dreary and wet, even the rosebuds rot. My hair has gone mud-blond in natural camouflage. Only the geese thrive to be eaten. The forests are bare, ordered and diseased. I miss the U.S. I look at ducks and I see Germans quacking.

My cousin Odo criticizes me. He thinks I am the strange one. I speak my native tongue in an American accent now.

It is true. I am an alien here. The *Ordnungsamt,* the Office of Order, is constantly redefining me. I have to get permits and permits, as if to breathe. The clerk called me a "border crosser."

I think of you. I think like an American, when I think of you.

Unfortunately my colleagues now are much like my cousin.

Odo hates English. "All the time like a snake hissing I would sound," he said. If he spoke English, he would be correcting mine at every turn. I showed him Anemone's picture of us, kissing over the party cake. He thought, that with your dark looks and as you are American, that you were an eagle-eyed Indian. I told him that you are Slavic and he spit. I told him, that his short nose comes from his Slavic grandmother and his blondness he owes to the Swedes. He cursed me, for, like a woman, telling the truth. I told him to go lick a light socket. He told me to go home, to America. I was pleased.

My most formative years were in the U.S. They came to fulfillment with you.

Oh, why did I ever come here? I had forgotten. I thought Germany, like me, had changed.

Day is a process of watching the light disappear. 'Gloomy Street 17' literally is my street address.

The studio is smaller than Odo promised, and the only window is the skylight, in the slant of the ceiling. But there is no sky, as you know it in San Francisco. It is only a fairy tale here.

Save me. My feet are so cold at night, that they wake me up. And I am suddenly allergic to my eye makeup. Please, please, save me.

Your love,
Sara

Dearest André,

Now the natives complain about the weather. No one wants to hear my complaints anymore. With so many complaining so much, I have less to complain about anyway, but I do complain because I like to complain. It is very Austrian.

Germans mostly complain about not being allowed to be German enough, by the rest of the world. Some few Germans complain that the country is too aware of its Germanness. They have problems. They demonstrate. Each year one dies, murdered, by the resenting proud.

The scientists I have known are many but they are no help in being. I once complained to my father, about my trouble not meeting a good man, and he told me how easily he found girlfriends. 'Of course, at my age I am not as picky,' he said.

My mother is my major complaint in life though (in my father's too I guess). I used to beat my dolls, punish them, be strict with them. I was awful with my cousins. My mother taught me levels and rank, but that she came first, and that I could do whatever I wanted to my friends, if I obeyed her. She would not even take me with her to the store when she bought my summer coats. She would just hand them to me and say, "Here!" She never listened to me cry or heard if I was sad. But we always traveled together, and complained together about the places we had been. That was fun.

But it is also why I went nine time zones away alone, to study, and why I dislike home so much. My father spends his spare time in caves. He has toured many of the very best in the world. Indeed he ran out of good ones long ago. Now he visits

Normandy bunkers and things like that. As I, he likes underground. He was on a submarine at the end of the war, the
last one, and was kept in a dungeon for a year afterwards, in
France. He has photographs of everywhere he has been, and a
girlfriend in each. I envy him his simple pleasures.

So-so, what are your secrets? Do you like mine?

Your love is very important to me, but I have one nagging
complaint about you. Since you don't listen, I will tell you
again. Do not anymore pat my behind, I'm a feminist!

If I could show you my dreams, I would. The skylight frame
casts a heavy shadow, but my dreams are light and clear and
loving, when I dream of you.

Once, before I met you, I visited Apple Computer and their
first all plastic building. It was radio-frequency-transparent, for
testing new hardware. You have made such a place unnecessary.
When I feel your presence, my world simply dissolves. Yes, yes,
your hardware penetrates my dreams, no matter how far apart
we are.

What do you dream?

Yours, in love,
S

Dear André,

Where are you?

I am in the new lab. It is less than the old one. Mr. Oxygen and Mr. Atmosphere, Walburt and Trudbert, are here visiting. The laser is lasing and I am taking data, finally. I wish I had nothing to do but to write to you, but this lab is quite difficult. Doing research in it means fighting equipment always.

Nix Geht, "Nothing Works," is our out-of-order sign.

Life outside is worse, more troublesome. To live well requires scrimping, bitching and making do. I am lost in this blue land, of tight laws and short measure. Sunday prohibitions last the week. Store hours are strictly regulated, in the name of social freedom. Soap in the laundromat is measured for you. Eggs are ten to the box, a liter of water is .7. Gastric despair is regional though. In this city, the rose hip jam smells like tomato paste. Turkey tastes like styrofoam. Even alive it is already processed. Egg yolks are dyed bright orange. Untouched, they remind me of old chewing gum. Yes, yes, they are thorough here, but I have yet to find a milk carton that easily opens. Germany is the most curious myth of itself. Why does anyone else believe in it? Even Germans can not afford their own arrogance. My father buys French for the better value. He can. He travels. Then again, it is difficult to be poor here, unless you are Turkish. It is equally impossible to become rich, unless you are a weasel or a political skunk.

But I am here and have to live. I need to buy a car, to shop, to eat. What would you do, Mr. San Francisco?

There are syrupy yams and fine citrus, imported from Israel, but costly. Everything from outside is. The *New Yorker* is $350 a year at the newsstand. I looked. (Do you still view the cartoons? I have trouble understanding yet. Is the person speaking always the one with his mouth open?)

Oh yes, there is carbohydrate if I want to get gross, yes, yes, marzipan treats and fresh seed bread on every corner. Odo asked me why all Americans are fat. I told him, that those are the ones who come from here.

I worry now, without you the only exercise my body gets is by eating. I feel like I am falling apart. This morning I pulled out of the shower drain enough hair to form a braid.

Worse, holiday decorations went up today in stores. They depress me endlessly. Christmas always makes me want to be Jewish. Walburt showed me an *El Al* ad, "Imagine a world without Christmas: It's as close as Israel!" Could we convert together?

Trudbert grew up near the American Army base here. When U.S. soldiers went into the woods on survival maneuvers, they would find him waiting and send him into town secretly, for beer, cigarettes and pastries. Trudbert earned plenty of *pfenning* when 11 years old. West Germany has done well through American indulgence. After all, life could be as dismal as East German existence is. I am 48 miles from the border. Americans are heroes on this side, in more ways than I want to imagine.

When my *Chef,* the chief at the lab, introduced me to my research group, he said he hoped that I would inspire my colleagues with the American work ethic that I have adopted. Yes, he did.

But I hang out in the coffee room as much as anyone, and I also now quit at quitting time. My colleagues here limit themselves to their job definition and salary hours. In the U.S. we lived in the lab, day and night. Trudbert and Walbert instantly reverted to type here too, but I feel guilty.

Meanwhile I have to go to the Office of Order again tomorrow, or I will not exist. I wish I did not sometimes. The lab here will look good on my resume, but its level of science is truly limited. Its best people are imported. Japanese are being invited by the bus-load, and Russians too. Even I am Austrian.

What Germany has in its favor is that it still makes industrial scale equipment precisely, like tanks for Iraq, poison gas plants for the Libyans, and such...

What can I alone do? I do not even know which is worse, if I open the lab windows, in a sunlit moment, to let the ozone in or out?

Sometimes I wonder about a new career, in a feminine-friendly science, deciding earth policy perhaps, but my mother never taught me to be a woman, only to study. My doctorate does not deflate you though, does it? Just how much of a masculinist are you anyway?

Where are you, my love? Who are you really? Women are said to have special ways of knowing, all their own. I wish that I knew what they were.

Ciao,
Sara

Dear Sara,

Three letters from you today. Underneath the complaints
I sense the promise. Can't you return? Why not? If you've made
a mistake, why don't you correct it? Isn't it a bigger mistake to
stay? Definitely it is! I'll tell you a story. Not long.

Before the earthquake, the German consulate in San
Francisco, at great expense, installed shielding inside its waiting
room walls, to mute the effects of a drive-in bomb. The con-
sular chief proudly insisted on before-and-after photographs,
to show everything looking exactly the same, condescendingly
comfortable, and corridored with rules, without a trace of steel
showing. It's the same in your fatherland, I'm sure. The government game is to hide the armor plate, the iron order surrounding any and all reception space. But you can see that too.

I'm afraid, that if you stay where you are, bars of endless
order will lock you from me and yourself as well in time, and
no dynamite of love will free you. How can I help you from
here? "The only thing definite is that I'm leaving," you said.
What's definitive is that you're gone.

For the photographer, who the consulate hired, I built a
special corner-camera from a redwood cigar box, to hold an
extreme wide-field lens. I fashioned a horizontal split-back as
well. The photographer needed only one sheet of film to make
the comparison and the deception obvious.

That was then. Now the quake has crumbled my livelihood.
Since, I haven't sold a single camera — except to you, of course.
The truth is, it doesn't take a custom model to photograph
wreckage. An Instamatic will show an empty lot just fine and
make it look even emptier. The problem is, I don't do mending.
Repair's the name of the game at the moment. Granted, my
expenses were cut in half by the loss of my flat, but even I had

to visit the audio technician upstairs on the hill, for help with
my stereo. He poked, probed, sniffed — stuck his nose against
the transformer, and the screwdriver in his ear — and then idly
explained his cello playing. He's always wanted a fine instrument. Now, instead, he's looking to electronics, Neo-Mesmo
and Slink, as the next new wave in music. Unlikely, I say.

In fact, he failed to fix my stereo. To console me and given
his change in taste, he offered me his opera ticket for the season
opener. I took it but never went in. The scene outside seemed
the better show. It fit my mood. False alarms summoned four
fire engines. A huge fur-covered woman fell down drunk. Six
firemen struggled to raise her again. The real Mr. San Francisco
— an elegant jeweled white-haired man — arrived in a cream-
colored limo, but a wiry black chauffeur had to lift him out
and into his wheel chair. In the midst of the tuxedoed crowd,
a Marine Corp veteran with camouflage face stood at silent
attention, on guard as it were in another dimension, holding
an inscribed "POW/MIA" flag, to remind us not to forget them.
Suddenly a tall slender young blond collapsed in pain on the
opera house steps. In new boots she'd run across town, not to
be late. The fire chief sent his handsomest fireman to cut off
her silk stockings at the ankles and dress her bloody heels.

I wish I could invent a culture-seeking camera without
moving parts, a kind of crystal ball, as it were, forever fixed to
now, to us, so we could show our separate lives to each other.
Definitely, an event-seeking camera, though it's impossible to
study culture in the realest sense — culture is between you and
me. We should be together.

At your party, you introduced me by saying, "He's past
30 and still being an artist. God!" — as if I were unbelievably
childish.

That remark still rattles me. Mine's a specialty craft, my

dear, not an art. In practice each camera serves an expert's purpose. Art is arbitrary. My cameras aren't.

Normally, I have to admit, I've a secret technical advantage. It's the reason my eyes look strangely. I'm far sighted in one and near-sighted in the other. My eyes make me see, in curious compensatory ways. I'll need glasses less as I age. The faults will reverse. Consequently I test my camera lenses close-up, and let infinity take care of itself, the reverse of the normal practice.

No, I don't make much money usually, but if there's art, it's in my improvisations for living. I do get tired of working with dental tools all the time and only taking an assistant's pay, but I'd use toothpicks to build my cameras if I had to. They're my pleasure. With you I feel that my lenses at last have seen something that I alone couldn't have. Your shyer side? Your hidden self?

One day, when your love erases the distance now between us, I'll tell you about the 180-degree camera I built on contract for a NASA mission, to help X-ray the nearest stars.

I love you, my dear,
André

Dear André,

So, you were born strange. That is your secret. No wonder
I am sometimes weird to you. Now I know. I am normal, my
eyes too. Can I see the way you do? Do I want to? Our lives
are so different. Will you make me part of yours? I only
show people the studio portrait you posed me for, with the
Gundlach. Both my second cousin Frowin and my father said
I looked so in focus that they did not recognize me. Am I
changing? Are you changing me? You do not have to deny
being an artist. You can be. I do not mind.

    I am sorry. I can not return. It is too late to rearrange my
life. There would be a year missing in my resume. I can not say,
"1990: Discovered Love." What would we have done if I had
stayed?

    Here, Frowin has joined the out-of-focus students, in
the *Autonome Szene.* The police killed two of his scene while
"protecting" it. There are big demonstrations now, but it is so
bitter cold, I stayed inside.

    My apartment is a wreck, but it is my doing. Maybe I
will clean this weekend, or buy some plants to hide things.
I like jungle.

    You would fit right in here. With your wild hair, and the
wire style of your special glasses, you already look like a rebel
student.

    However, you did not answer my other questions. Tell me,
would you convert for me? And what planet do *you* live on?

I love you anyway,
Sara

Dear Sara,

Tell me more of your secrets first. Mine aren't that unusual.
When I was your age I used to figure out the craziest ways to
blow up the world. But that's normal. I've learned how, too.
Photography is language, and the chemistry of light, but I get
to play with explosive substances, poisons and precious metals
in the process. Also, instead of teaching you, I'm relearning
photography myself. The earthquake set me free. Definitely!

If you'd stayed we'd be married and living happily ever
after, I suppose. And we'd be traveling together, for sure.

If you're serious about converting, I'd consider it. I always
liked the command, "Go forth and multiply!" Was it meant
for individuals or society as a whole?

Normally I'm not much of anything. Cinema's the worship
of choice these days, music videos mostly. Even the blind could
tell you that. But photography's a religion too. Its temples are
the museum gallery, the news-rack, bank walls, terminals, and
the billboard road. But that could be changing. Who knows? I
thought I did, till the earthquake unmade my beliefs.

I wish I could tell you what to do. Should I find new ways
to annoy you, since you take such pleasure in complaining?

Living with my cameras, surrounded night as well as day,
intensifies my dreams. They're more enjoyable now, more real
and stay with me longer, as if I've photographed them. They
reach back before you, mostly.

It's not as impossible without you as I thought it'd be.
Surprised, my dear? What new and challenging there?

Love,
André

The surprise is on you. The Berlin Wall is falling, and my period just began. I have been worried. Are you disappointed? I hope not. The government may be though. It has had a campaign going, extending payments for new mothers from 12 to 18 months, so women will reproduce more, and to keep them at home. Education money, it is called. Yes, yes, teach women their place, pay them in halves. As it is, school ends at noon, forcing a *Hausfrau* to finish her shopping early, get to the house-cleaning and stop thinking of freedom. "Have a Baby" billboards surround the town.

Forgive my handwriting. I am on the train to Berlin, to meet my parents. They are already there. This is an exciting moment in the history of Germany. I doubt you share it, but the breaks in the wall thrill everyone here, myself included.

The fall of the wall will stop the blood flowing. Still, the birth of freedom will mean the end of our pretense to innocence. Yes, yes, business as usual will soon prevail, but idealism is alive for now. The liberation of East inspires us in the West also. Yet, the government here already is poised to impose itself there. "There must be order," I hear again and again; '*Ordnung ist alles*,' '*Kontrolle ist besser*' are the headline reality of every ordinary day. But for the moment hope and joy are everywhere that there is not indifference. East Germany is the newborn now, 18 million at once. Welcome shoppers, relatives, Germans!

I have always liked trains. You never know who you will meet. I brought books to read nonetheless. My favorite stories have always involved a trip and a treasure. But Espionage is irrelevant now that the wall is pierced. And Romance is usually unreal. Mysteries too have never been dear to me. The form is absurd. It proposes a simple criminal agent. It begs the question of death, by making one answer: Man. Death is a dangerous puzzle only to the unscienced. Really, death is life. Am I being morbid? I am. It must be the window view. The gray, barren, third-world waste of East Germany looks so raped and raw. It's untraveled in the touring book that I bought. The only gold waiting at the Berlin Station will be my father's pocket watch.

Yes, yes, there is the media view and the immediate view. Where are you, which are you? Are you as real as I want you to be for me? I hope so, I love you so. Or have you only fallen in love with my picture, your pictures of me?

Want to hear a feminist joke? Do you know what a vampire's teabag is? Of course you do, it's a tampon!

I still like the train. It started my period.

- -

Hallo, my dear, as we so often say here.

The return train is full. The five Dutchmen in my compartment are rowdy and drunk and I can not sleep.

Berlin is still fascinating, you would enjoy it. It's chaotic though, which is fun, but getting places is complicated — unless you have a rich daddy leading the way. My parents enjoy showing off Berlin and acting as if it were the first time for them too. It is not, for any of us. In spite of our family name we are not natives, but we like to think that we are, and used to come here often. The places of my childhood memory are mostly gone or dilapidated now, but East Berlin seems much richer and friendlier. The main impression from my last trip, in 1979, were the ruins. This time we hardly found any. I regret that earlier I barely took any pictures, to document my feelings, (I was even shyer than now back then).

My great grandmother survived the war here. The place
where she lived survives her. It looks so much like the massive
apartment building in Vienna where I grew up, with an airy
view to a stone courtyard, that we got very sentimental. My
original home in Vienna remains a timeless island of domestic
happiness and family remembrance.

Berlin is different really. A very intense place always,
it is now the focus of many Germans. The pictures I took are
already historic. The wall continues to fall. Cutting a hole in it
was an act of enormous political significance for Europe. The
fuss around it has turned tasteless though. Much alcohol, broken glass and dirt, rowdiness at the Brandenburg Gate at night,
mobs of tourists (including many foreigners) during the day,
to see the scene that they are themselves creating. Some are
jack-hammering the best art from the wall into pieces. The
souvenir trade is booming. Everybody takes pictures, everybody the same ones, I am afraid. It was still interesting to
watch, especially East and West meeting, many for the first
time, and simply asking each other questions.

Though the wall is almost down, a chain link fence went
up in its place, with innumerable check-points to pass through.
The East soldiers stare through the wire at their medals and
uniforms for sale in the West, the same that they still proudly
wear. For ten Mark I bought a Russian Army hat, in the largest
size. Hopefully it fits you.

My father gave me my great grandmother's hand-written
recipe book. Now I can make gooseberry jam for you for the
holidays. I would like to go next week again to Berlin, without
my parents. Will you come with me?

Good night, my love (the drunks fell asleep before me).

Sara

Dear Sara,

Berlin? For the weekend? Should I pack rocket launchers? Are
there electronic game parlors at least to play in?

If I convert, can I also claim a garden in East Berlin? Is this
our chance? Sorry, but I'd rather grow grenades than German.
You should know, my family's experience planted the seeds in
me pretty deeply. The flower of antagonism is still feeding.

So you intend to revisit the "lovefest," as the *Times* called it.
Alone? By taking your vacation without me? Did I release your
energies and turn you loose? Should I balance the scale, spend
a weekend at the latest hot spring? Have fun, my dear! I may
too. Here the white buffalo is on the loose. If your life is there,
mine's still here, but I'm half-willing — to check on your alien
views. Does the scene need a witching? I know what to do.

Really you're rather far for a 2 day trip. Your science
interests me, but not the scientists. What happens if I come,
and I'm lonelier with you than without you? Who's around
when you're labbed-in?

Do you realize then, that when I leave, I'll be leaving you?

Tell your father to fly here instead and bring his lost little
daughter with him. I'm by myself now in my darkroom cave,
though my shades are up again. Nili looked in yesterday and
asked to engage me, to film a wooden match head, that she'd
etched with a laser as a heat test. She offered to pay me in
poems, "in silver flame". Those were her words.

Am I the only person you still speak English to?

U.S. media is reliving the defeat of Germany in 1945.

Your personal partisan,
André

Your letters distress me. How can you dislike this country so much? Why do you love me anyway? Isn't it because I am a foreigner? Which half of you wants to come?

You Americans always pursue the impossible! Probably if I were a wonky Australian, you would love me equally. Are you this way with everyone? I want to know, who is the woman on your wall? Am I her all over again? You will explain yourself. Your letter upset me greatly. I am very ordinary here. I doubt myself, but I believe in us. Do not destroy my faith. You have no reason to be jealous.

Also, I hardly appreciate your remarks about my father. Nor would he. I am not my parents, or anyone's past.

And I do not like your camera. Maybe it listens to you, but it does not to me. What did you tell it? My pictures from Berlin are all wrong. The lens warped the falling wall into barrels. Do I need two wrong eyes to see right, through your cameras?

If we married, would you glue your name to me also?

I want you here. I need you. You can do here what you do there? What is a year? Do you have anything better to do, than flirt with Nili?

I still love you. Why do you love me?

Take care,
Sara

Dear Sara,

A negative woman always comes out positive in the darkroom.
I spent Friday night dipping you in selenium and ferrocyanide,
to alter the contrast and tone of your portrait. Nili watched,
without a word, amazed at my mania.

Guess I don't like being in the dark about you. Sorry if my
questions cut to the heart of the matter too quickly. But why
make me jealous if you don't mean to? And why look for a
party to celebrate Germany? You know the price we'll all pay
later. That's for sure.

I'm at the Marina Green now, center of the quake scene.
It's been 2 months, yet the picture's the same — ground split,
gates up, most houses dark, the roadway rippled, police
swarming, runners racing blindly ahead, not sight-seeing.
People learn to live with the damage so easily. The area's still
roped off, to all but the residents. You'd never know I once
lived here. My place has vanished, a camera can't bring it
back. You're gone also, but I stare at your photograph and
see more than I know, of myself and you. Sure, I've fallen in
love with your portrait. Still, you're a thousand photographs
I've yet to make. But I can only make them one at a time, to
show you as you are.

The woman, who you saw on my wall, was a ceramicist.
She thought in bleached-bone clay. She styled beautiful snow-
scenes. One day she vanished, poisoned by the mercury of a
very white glaze. I found her in Napa, where she remains, in
a locked room, though she may be out soon. Sure, I love her
still, as a photograph. You're nothing like her. She was always
a silent self-absorbing shape and deeply Scandinavian.

To photograph the collapses in the Berlin wall, you need

a panorama camera, designed for the purpose of walls. Look for a vintage original, in your neighborhood perhaps. Find one for me too, though I already have five. Should I bring four there? You could photograph the fat lady in the circus then as well.

If I offered my name and it stuck to you somehow, it'd be an accident, I'm sure — like the name itself. When my father, Mikhail Illych Opticon, came to the U.S., immigration called him Mike Apple. My dad went along gladly, to hide from his first 2 wives. Besides, the Opticon was my grandfather's invention. He pioneered a revolving show — a pre-motion picture device. No one is quite sure of its workings. When WWI came, my grandmother buried her every-day dishes, not her husband's exotic toys. His were lost with him. I simply revived the name, shortened, in hopes of living up to it. Why would you want it?

Did I say something about your father?

Save you? Or will I lose myself?

Life is and should be a merry-go-round. To you, it's a fault line. Isn't it?

Am I wrong? No? Come back to me then. In spite of Germany, the Russian gene pool hasn't dried up, so I'll admit my temper, and my intemperance. But don't splash the happy water, and I won't have to shout out for help. Who's to save me?

Love,
André

Dear André

It is not as bad here, as I have led you to believe. Europe has settled down now. There is peace. I will not go anywhere again, till we can go together. I stayed home this weekend for you. But it would be good for me to travel. I am getting computer nose again. It runs constantly. Also, smoking caused my hard drive to self-destruct. I hung the mangled remains on the wall. In the U.S. it would be a trophy. Here it was recycled within an hour.

You should arrange an e-mail address, so I could reach you instantly. You are my mirror without meaning to be. Yes, yes, your cameras show me as I am. I know they do but why will they not obey me? And why must I take your name?

About my father, you can not say anything at all, until you have met him. Meanwhile, my mother is still married to him, poor woman.

I am worried about us. Please ease my doubts.

Lovingly,
Sara

Dear Sara,

Till we've our own place, my home is still in you, wherever you are. We narrowed the space around us so well. No matter what the size of the bed, we always woke up that close.

You're only alien to me because you went away. Okay?

I love you,
André

I haven't gone anywhere either, and am paying the price also. My head burns, off and on. I've nausea — too much time in the darkroom with ever more dangerous chemicals.

My reality now is a dream of you. Deep in my eyes, I see you, no picture before me, in the brightness of day. Your eyes lighten the dark also. You enchant me.

Your portrait dreams as well. I watch it dreaming. I wonder, does it embrace me? I've no idea what it sees. The chemicals split the tones into different colors, and then blend them together again.

I might try uranium intensifier next, to increase the range, but it's a triple poison inhaled. The sulfurs I breathe are bad enough. Definitely!

Has an hour passed? I'm still in the darkroom, sweating, vague, listless. I wonder if hunger, a bad tooth, or the heavy metals are experimenting with me. I was dreaming of you, as an expert in 12 waters. Now I've visions of the ice blue lights, of the police cars on earthquake night.

My cave gets more colorful all the time, though I think black and white tells your story best, without translation. You're in my eyes forever now, asleep or awake.

Time to gethefukout of here, need air.

Why are you smoking?

I love you,
André

Dear André,

I am nervous, I smoke. I do not know what the future will be.
I wish we were in no-space and no-time, just the two of us together. There is a 1000 year old house near here that fascinates
the American in me. It would be dear to you too, no?

I realize the trouble we are having now is my fault. I left
you. I did. I know that. How awful of me, but every new chance
for us now charms the day.

The second time we met, you happened for me, completely.
Suddenly it was as if we were running at each other as fast as
possible, not to lose one minute of the few we had. It felt like
you made me take the steps toward touching. You did without
words. You offered everything to me. It is still hard to believe
that we are really happening. I had given up. I never have
experienced romantic love so deeply. You broke the ice in me.
You healed so many of my old wounds so quickly. I remember
what my father used to say, 'When the right man rises, you will
shine with him.' As simple as that. It is wonderful. The clouds
are gone. I feel embarrassed. I never told you, but I have worried that I show too much affection, that you will think I am
acting ridiculous in overdoing myself. Now I realize it is okay
to allow my feelings. Do I? Enough? Can you really know that
I love you?

Do you remember the first night, when you did not sleep
at all and bravely claimed you did not need any? I was afraid
you would lose interest, get bored with me. I thought you
might, as so many do, go out of your way at first, to reel in the
catch, for sport, then let go, but the honeymoon lasted. It's my
fault it got interrupted. We need to be married. Will you marry
me? When?

Love, Sara

Hi Sara,

Nili says I shouldn't give you a hard time if I love you. But a 1000 year old house needs a 1000 years of repair. I want tall open walls, not in need of bracing, a future not a past, with the sunrise always in view. Can you show that to me?

Nili came back with a poem that she wanted me to photograph. That is, she wanted a picture of herself reading, at a darkly-lit culture center in the no-man's land between Pacific Heights and the Fillmore, managed by Horst and Sigrid, guest revolutionary poets on the run from West Germany. I don't know why. But I brought three rolls of the newest film that sees in the dark — T-Max 3200, it can be used at 32,000 ASA. I built a camera for the film, with an 0.9 lens — beyond the theoretical limit. Unfortunately it didn't illuminate the poem, or catch the cracks in Nili's voice. Her eyes glowed. Definitely. Only they were in focus. She dedicated her words to us. The meanings escape me:

> *"Photo bacteria squirm, to genetic loopholes.*
> *Chromosomes   quirk, decay into visible light.*
> *Her default drive is   set. His probe molecules*
> *optically bond her energy   wells. Her hyperfine*
> *quenching   now a cyanide sunset is his screen*
> *saver. She can park his head from a foot   to*
> *infinite.   His proton pump encourages more*
> *collision-induced   relaxation...."*

I don't remember the rest. It was longer than your shopping list. She says the poem's unfinished anyway and always will be but it's about optically forbidden transitions. Maybe you know what she means. *"dir b: the anomaly of impossible numbers"*, she called it.

I met her husband. He's the square root of normal squared, surprisingly. He asked to buy my shop. I told him he could have it for a new Nikon F6. Curiously, he said it's worth many orders of magnitude more. I'm not so sure. Is he also a scientist, in disguise? Like her, he's small with a large voice.

Dinner followed the reading. Nili brought cardboard lunchboxes stamped "courtesy of Dow Chemical", leftover from their recruiting visit to you. Thin cheese sandwiches, tasty still.

After eating on the floor of the culture club, the audience cheered the announcement that the Red Army Faction had successfully exploded Deutsche Bank chairman, A. Herrhausen. Yes, the man of the house, and an easy mark these days. Are you aware? Were many Germs infected by the news? I suspect Horst and Sigrid were here to establish alibis.

Since, I've been wondering how much disruption pays. Is the risk too great? I'll need a new support system to get me to you.

Your still-hungry lover,
André

It's me again. Fortune smiles. Luckily, happily, our Japanese friends are buying old chrome cameras now, as well as Van Goghs. One natty little man announced himself to be famous in his own country, as a wedding photographer, and purchased my father's Zorki, a rangefinder model, engraved by the NKVD. It back-focuses badly. This guy didn't care. He bought the camera's history at 5 times its replacement value.

Immediately, from the rear of my shop I dragged out my dad's suitcase, a one-piece stressed-leather immigrant original, that my father brought with him 60 years ago. I've been saving it for the next rummage sale at the Russian Center. Broken jewelry sold for 50 cents a cup at the last sale. Russians enjoy rummaging, they can look so rummaged themselves. My dad once worked in a camera factory near Moscow, making view cameras. The Deardorf lookalike in my window was his. Inside the suitcase was the broken jewelry of his trade — flint glass, cracked prisms, stripped gears, brass sleeves, cherrywood veneer, retaining springs. My dad saved everything, including his best work, for himself. He always said, "Quality exists in Russia, in what you make for your own." I sold the contents of the suitcase to the wedding photographer also, suggesting that it was what was left of the photo industry in Port Arthur in 1905, after the Japanese destroyed the Russian Navy there. Too bad. I was only 4500 miles from the truth.

Could I find more, similarly-valuable suitcases in Eastern Europe, now that it's opening up? Does your father know of unopened caves used for hiding? Haunted even, but trophied, and with an anxious price? It hadn't occurred to me before, that the useless and lost could command such high rates when the story is right. The ale men will find out too, but I'd like to ferret around before they do.

In fact I wouldn't mind touring the museums also. In England in the last century one lord covered his box camera with his wife's skin. She complained so much about his passion for photography that, after she died, he had her flayed. His revenge is now on display. Malady doesn't always make for invention, but the camera fascinated my father. Still, like many Russians of his time my father admired the French more, for their healthier excesses, but France had no room for him, when it came to setting up shop. Its photographic community was already brilliant and denied his work permit. The U.S. didn't.

Can you put your politics aside, and let me know what's now to be found, and how dear or difficult the finding will be, at least in German countries?

I wish my father were still alive — so does he — he might be able to show me the way. I'm the first and only son of his third marriage. Whether war has left any relatives still living, east of you, I haven't a clue.

Realistically I'll have to close my shop and cash in my stocks to get to you. Yesterday in memory of my inheritance, I went to a Chrysler shareholder's meeting here in San Francisco and listened to Lee Iococca, the CEO, cheerlead the monied into still believing. After all, Chrysler sold almost 4000 wheels in Japan last year. My father willed me his certificates but took the dividends with him. My car, his car, a New Yorker, barely runs.

Should I be trading my camera-craft and struggling stocks, my father's legacy, for our wedding pictures? Thanks to your Germany and its wars, I have no other inheritance.

Maybe it's time to excavate in your neighborhood, to find the veins in the bedrock again. Or is it smarter to travel more lightly, with just a can-opener attitude, and let the worms loose? At least, there'll be fishing.

Love, André

Dear André,

You are terrible. Europe grows together. Why can't we?

I went with my Papa again to the DDR. There are thirty new political parties in East Germany now. Unification is the common theme. The world is changing. Can't we, for each other? Please come visit me. You need a German lesson anyway, without apology.

I told my father about us. He approves and agrees that you are the best man for me. There is astronomy and there is life, he said. He told me, that now he can divorce my mother. I was shocked. He said, his life was not over either. He asked jokingly if I had a love-souvenir for him too. He likes Americans. He gets sentimental over canned California peaches, our favorite post-war luxury. I asked him about caves with hidden treasures for you. He told me of his.

Near my home in Vienna there is an abandoned mine, under a lake. The mine is normally flooded. During the war he helped seal the bottom of the lake, then pump out the mine for a Messerschmidt factory. We made war planes like fine knives. Yes, yes, my father knows of many hidden caves. Your government did too. The lake was bombed unmercifully by the British and Americans during the war. Indeed they were always dropping their unused bombs on us, and destroying cultural resources. There is not much left, but we are rebuilding. You should look nearby. Anything found would be welcome, I am sure. You could restore it.

The U.S. still picks on my country, you know. It tells us who to vote for and what to export. My father does not care. He smokes Johnny cigarettes, an American blend of strong tobacco imported by Austria's state monopoly. After the war an American flag decorated the pack. Ten years ago the pack looked like a denim pocket. I smoke Dunhills. Everybody smokes something.

We traveled this time to out-of-the-way places in East Germany. I love architecture. Cities have molecular structure in the ring road of life. I also love ruins. I identify with them. I hope now that they are not all repaired. But it would be nice if someone cleaned off the coal dust.

We stayed in horrible hotels without service. One night just before dinner, half the staff fled to the West. The cook became busboy, waiter and cashier and could have cared less. We had to wait so long on line to eat, there was only one meal left. The room had no shower or toilet. I washed my hair in a sink smaller than my head.

When I got back I bought a mustard Mercedes, with pumpkin interior, for us. Children line the road all day to wave to them in the DDR, our abbreviation for East Germany. You should see there too. You will learn.

Love,
Sara

Dear Sara,

Last night I decided. Definitely! Today I decided once more, to join you in two weeks for two months. Ready for me? For us? Again?

I've been washing my hair in the sink also, and pushing my car off the hill to start it...I might as well be with you...Each day another day's lost to thinking of you...I'm slowly packing up shop...You may have to come to get me yet. There are things within things within things here. I can't believe what hiding I'm given to. There are treasures unseen here. I hope I find some there...Regardless, I love you...so I still write, to get you to. I still love, for your love. I still want, for your need. There's only the darkroom now, to make you new. I wish we were always in bed, deeply together, closely wet...I'm thrilled to a standstill just thinking of you. Erect against my will. What should I do?...Into the darkroom, back to the well, to draw out your silver from its dry gel?...Why does your father think I'm so right for his lovely, loving daughter? Is he as competitive as you?... Nili's husband bought my lease, he's retiring my sign — The Optical Apple is now Optik Antiks. He's restocking the shop with holograms, prisms, crystals and pseudo-laser lights, trinkets really, tourist toys. He said, you must have good bed-time stories to tell, to get me to give up here. No, I said, I'm simply putting everything in storage and hoping to bring back more.

But I'm running out of time here. I'd better move... Leaving's too soon. Perhaps there'll be some good good-byes before I'm gone — onward to see you....

Always,
André

Dear André,

I want to tell you wonderful things too, instead of the bla-bla,
yet every time again I rush to the post office with whatever I
have written. Then I remember things, memories I want to
share, little stories about when I was a child. Nothing special,
there is nothing exciting in my life, except going away from
Austria. The only time I get homesick is when I go home, when
the train rolls into the western end of the city. It is familiar and
alien at once. I belong there, yet I do not. I always wanted to
leave, to travel as far away as possible. and yet it still hurts to
leave. My mother is wide in figure but stuck in her narrowness.
I rebel against her mind with all my might, but my strength is
finite. I pity her. I admire her. I despise her. The women around
her are weaker than she is. Maybe she depends on them to be. I
try to teach her feminism, but it is too late in her life. It will be
good for you to meet, for her to see us together, happy and sad.
You are not very real to her. She is positive that you are one of
the *Terroristen* on the post office wall, without a disguise.

My father now, having decided his life is before him, ran
away with a nurse. How could he? Has he no pity?

It may please you to know that I was insulted by my close
colleagues. They read in the press about an extreme right wing
politician in Bavaria and they sniped at me in blame: 'Another
half-Austrian to get us into trouble!' Does that please you? But
the fault is not always on the other side of the fence. Have you
learned that yet?

Oh, this might be the last letter I write to you before you
come. I will miss writing to you. Life *is* so very strange. How
can it be? An old, old dream coming true! And yet everything

totally unexpected! You surprise me every time. Your love makes me float. I spin in the air with joy when a letter from you arrives. You are making me so happy. I hope I can do the same for you. I am always with you. I love you so much.

I am still nervous. I can not deny it. That is why I have been smoking again. I am not taking anything for granted. I am worried about you not liking it here, not finding challenges, or friends, or whatever — and being disappointed with me. What will I be able to do for you? I will try all I can, but I am weak. There is so much I do not know. I can not predict, but when you are here, you will make all the difference. Tell me what you think, what your needs are, how I can uplift you.

I do not really want to take the train to pick you up. I want to be alone with you, not a hundred people listening and watching. I still so much want to go to no-space and no-time with you, and only enjoy being together.

I am trying to imagine the day you arrive here. You should come tomorrow, no, yesterday. But it is so soon and wonderful.

Please keep writing in these last days.

Forever yours,
Sara

Dear Sara,

By the time you get this I'll already be there, birding you, bedding you, loving you — everywhere. Waiting for you to tell me what your letters couldn't, listening at the jungle in you, I'll kiss, hug and hold you till your cunt unfolds and opens to me. I'll feed at your lips, slide down your thighs — my Department of Disorder loves your sighs. And then I'll hear the resonance of your heat. And we'll sleep, and sleep, till I wake you again with my tongue...

Problems? Definitely, we'll have our share. The way we ease past them is what counts. Oh yes, the future's full of worries, if that's what you want, but our love lifts us, guides us, keeps us, during our time here, from any harm. So I sprain a finger, twist a knee, go without sleep now and then, in my rush to get to you. So you have a lover's light disease that you try to hide, a few nights of unease, a blemish or two from stress — all things heal, become our history, grow well. And we go on into now, flying together, two lovers, one love. Your energy of calculation dissolves. My vision clouds. For sure, we will share the same dream of now, to blend and fit so perfectly, a new seed sprouts. Let it. I love you....

André

Dear André,

Though you will not read this letter, I had to write once more.
How can I let you know, I am so frightened — Why can't I hear
your thoughts? You are so Russian after all, falsely practical, a
romantic, a poet, yet a salesman too. Still I'm waiting again for
you to reach out to me. I feel the same happy tension now as
before. My body wants yours, to touch me all over, kiss my lips,
my hair, my breasts, suck on me, I want you between my legs,
come inside, as deeply as you can — I'm ready for you always,
to penetrate me, dissolve me. Yes, yes, explore me, every day
newly, turn me over, upside down, anyway you can think of,
but stay with me as close as you can, inside me. Teach me how
I can ecstacize you. I want to feel us unite again and again. Give
me glory. Give my country back its strength. We need your
eyes, as strange as they are, to help us see, for me to see myself,
to make ourselves be seen the way we rightly are, so that we
may live again, fully, openly, proudly.

Do I dare tell you, how important you are to me, to us?
Do you know? You have so many dreams. Will I choose the
right one, for you, for us?

Yes, yes, you have woken things in me that were hidden,
submerged, disallowed. As they come out, they create new
flaws in me, *ja, ja,* they do. I need your encouragement and
trust now more than ever I thought I would. I wonder about
the future alot, but can not predict. My ambitions depend
so much on you. I am afraid — because I do not understand.
What is happening to the U.S., that it is letting Germany
become a country again? Have you failed yourselves? That is
what we wonder here. Odo believes you could not help but

stumble in your purpose because your population is so mixed
with the people we did not want and chased out. I tell him,
that is your strength, but I am not sure.

You must never know how much I love you, yet at the same
time I fight my biology. Love is not enough.

But I must know, why are you coming? Why are you letting
us win, after defeating us so badly?

Is it for a German lesson? Or to give us one? To defeat us
again?

If it is only for cameras, my father will guide your search,
to its goal. When I was younger I loved the attention of my
father during photographs. You are like him, you know, you
concentrate so completely. I feel that I am still growing up,
that I will heal soon. Do you know your effect on me? Do you
care?

You must. You are coming. It is a dream come true.
I want to write to you in the sky with my laser, and excite
the stratosphere, your love lases me so.

Scheisse, I am getting wet for nothing.

Lovingly,
Sara

Dearest Sara,

Yesterday I said good-bye to a my favorite sights, to a coastal redwood grove, to the crookedest street, to an ocean-carved cave in the soapstone-ribbed shore.

San Francisco was tall in fog, its soft pastel towers reaching through the mist, reflecting on the bay in the low late sun, as the plane arced north.

I'm sitting next to a sprawling fleshy sleeper, coming from her father's second funeral. She declared him dead once before, it would seem. She's a feature writer for a women's fanzine in Seattle, my first layover on this flight to you.

London's the second. I discovered that I've an aunt there, but I'm still all yours. In fact this letter will be hand-delivered. I'll be my own postman, flying an air stream nine-time-zones-wide. No more snail-mail for us for awhile.

The woman next to me also said her good-byes yesterday, but she doesn't let go, of what's in her teeth, at least. Through a mouthful of chocolate mousse, she told me, "San Francisco, yuck, it molests itself. It's infested with viruses, obsessed with pesto, and possessed by its fog, so much so that —" She broke off in a choking cough.

Can you suppose? Did she nip her father's bones clean? San Fran's whatever you want it to be. I hope to bring you back to the fun, but I can introduce you to anywhere else you might want, including the simple life of happily ever after. My dream is private space, a driftwood fireplace, a view with no one in it but rippling water that reflects the sky. Indeed I enjoy spending as much time as I can in the canyon woods, and up the steeper coasts. No, you'll never be barefoot and pregnant in a farm kitchen. Yet, to escape the city, I've let my life weave across the countryside, to anchor with the boats, and root with the trees.

You haven't seen this part of me. I haven't either in a while.

But now, inside, my eyes light to your burning, my pen dances with your flame, however dim in the distance. Yes, if my pictures speak, if these words see, it's because you're my new window to dreams.

Strange, how sitting next to death inspires living.

Stranger still is that alone and knowingly I'm flying into a dark warp, a winter night, your night. My shop's empty, the plywood walls are bare, the skylight's painted closed, the magic there is gone. It's in you now. I sold my sign gladly and left everything behind. Pruning the vine of entanglement does create a new view, but I don't see yet where we're going.

Promise me that one day we'll build our own home.

I've a more immediate concern. Here you had flexible hours. Definitely. There you're locked in as though on a time card. I'll have my slot too, it seems, I'll be punched into place as well. Can we change this? Or shouldn't I worry?

To minimize jet lag, I've had no coffee today, but now a headache's brewing. I must be as addicted as you. Perhaps it's my time to go through withdrawal, to find what I really need, in the raw —

The lights on the plane just dimmed. The seatbelt sign's on. Guess I'll turn in. I hope when I wake I'll be saying hello to you and us all over again.

Your lover,
André

CET (Central European Time)

Lieber Papa !

This letter will introduce my new lover. He is a difficult man, perhaps all the more important to me because of this. I write to you in English so that he will not think I am hiding anything from him or you. He refuses to learn German. In this he is most obstinate, and I tell him so at every opportunity, but it does no good. He is often ungrateful, irresponsible, and rude, but I believe he loves me as much as he likes giving me a hard time. He has been here with me for six weeks. I am sending him to you in Graz for help. He needs an income as well as manners. He is convinced that here there are rare photographic treasures to be found, that they will fall around him, as our walls continue to do. I have told him, that he must fend for himself, but I gave him my car, an old Mercedes that will not survive another TUV. The next inspection will reveal floorboard rust and remove the car forever off the road. He knows his cameras and lenses, better than even the laser and optics experts here. He has taught me subtractive and additive color, how to filter my UV laser toward visibility, and how to substitute quality camera equipment for the special scientific level that is many magnitude more in price but does not show equal advantage. He is a purist, a believer in simplicity, but in many simplicities. He knows how to take apart complex things and put them back together again. I do not. If you had been good with tools, I would also be, but I am afraid of them even as I use them. He is working on me as well I think. Yes, yes, he is smart enough to use your intelligence against you, if you let him. He is Russian by way of California, or rather a rebuilt Russian, with the work done in America. He has a hint of

French in his insolence. Sometimes I suspect he believes in nothing. I scold him, the way *Mutter* scolded you all the time. I hope this is not the way couples are supposed to behave throughout life. Perhaps you can get him to listen. If you introduce him to nurses, I will turn my lasers on you and reduce you both to blips on my screens. Forgive my insolence, but you were my teacher. If you need to know more, call me. We will talk, yes we will.

I did tell him about our family, more than I wanted. Things slipped out. He knows that you sacrificed artifacts of our past for my fare to study in the U.S., and that you helped me now, to bring back a double bed from the DDR, but he has the potential to replace your losses. He creates cameras that see the way things looked one hundred years ago. America owes us this, he knows, I have told him. He does not believe me. For now he sees only his purpose.

Please guide him, and he will help you in your need, possibly. Convince him! I have my own plans for him, but he resists. I will win him though.

Ja, Papa, he knows how to satisfy a woman.

Liebe Bussi !
Sara

Dear Sara,

I'm still in Graz, in the mountains, at an inn, on my way out.
I liked your father. He was amusing, without meaning to be.
I found him, casually at home, comfortable in retirement,
wrapping his seasonal present for your mother, a new book,
Hitler Won the War. Yeah, sure. He said, your mother was very
conservative, that she didn't believe in oral sex but that her
dumplings were perfect. He intended no irony — I think.
    I delivered your letter, which I hadn't read! On finishing
it he was all smiles. Given his seemingly open ease, I told him
directly, that I've come to see what's in the graveyard of Europe
— since the East's been the most dead, maybe something's still
buried there — a unique lens perhaps, that offers a new way of
seeing. I explained, that in the U.S. I've discovered every sort
of old camera, but here nothing. In fact, I asked, is the seed
pride of Europe scattered across the Atlantic entirely? Or do I
just need a guide? He said, I must narrow my range, limit my
enthusiasm, remain between the Rhine and the Danube.
I told him, I've already put 2,000 kilometers on the car. He
said, but the Soviet Union took most everything. Soldiers wore
a minimum of 5 watches on each wrist when they left. "If I
were Russian, would you blame the Americans?" I asked. His
eyes showed confusion as if unsure who I was. I drank his wine
and kept prodding, in an off-the-cuff manner. So, I told him,
maybe too frankly, "What I find in Austria, on my own, as
no one gives directions here, is simply — hulking resentment,
inflexible envy, and the dry constipations of an angry culture."
He replied with a curt smile: "Why expect more?" That was
his entire answer. Later he politely showed me his limited
stamp collection — the Hitler-faced 100 million mark wartime inflation issues and similarly surcharged stamps meant for
occupied-countries, also overprinted with Adolph's likeness.

Your father, an imperialized runt himself in profile, excitedly pointed out the postmarks. (Similar stamps filled starter packs in the U.S., when I was a kid.) I think your father believes that we're still at war, but that we should enjoy being adversaries and even take pride in each other's victories. I told him that the human cost of his stamps was too high. He said, that was only because we, the Allies, resisted so hard. Definitely.

To my surprise, he drives a French car. The price was right, he said. "I am not disloyal," he explained, "With the Danish, I too believe that the French are also German, only with more style. The ooo-la-la factor, you would call it."

Much later, sobering over strudel and dark coffee your father unwrapped his own photographs. I was amazed. They were solid technical achievements, from an open dramatic eye — fireworks on New Year's, bat-lined caves, and the re-gilded musical grind of Vienna. Good stuff. As we were talking media, he told me that he once purchased 1,500 meters of 35mm film — of a former corporate executive, "very important, executed at Nürnberg" — to give in good will to the executive's company, but was never rewarded, much to his dismay. I asked then about special caves. He said, the caves are museums now, but bare mostly.

It's doubtful that he'll help me. In fact he said, he has no personal interest in knowing Eastern Europe beyond East Germany. However, if I want to open a photographic shop in Vienna, and bring my cameras there, he would stake me. "My Namibia plantation is in need of a manager also," he said. I no-thanked him. To me Vienna seems too much like a double-Y chromosome ward, incurable, unsightly, a mass of ugly cement. As for Namibia, it's famous for its hot dry winds, pygmy population, and harsh colonial past, which no one else wants to revive. I didn't know, that Namibia had once been a German colony. I wondered aloud, if your father wasn't working for the

Austrian Chamber of Commerce. Once he had, he said. I asked what Austria still has to sell the world, and he said, itself. It can't, I answered, as long as it re-elects past Nazi functionaries, like Waldheim, as its leader. He said, I was rather naive but that he has friends of every persuasion, even Rumanian. Then he refused to say more, except good night. In the morning, he told me, "Austria also has Alps, and they are a-political."

Perhaps but they're losing their snow, I answered. "We are the mountains of Germany nonetheless," he said proudly.

I hope, I think we got along, in our own way, by not taking each other too seriously. He's pleasantly inoffensive compared with the other grimacing menaces here.

Yes, using a table napkin as cover, I photographed a few of the rigidly twisted faces in Vienna's Museum Cafe. Looks to me like the city needs a new Freud. Sigmund would shit, knowing he's now on the Austrian $5 bill, building small egos. I explored his museum. Really it's the Fraud Museum. There's nothing but anxious guards and photographs of what Freud took with him to London when he escaped with his life. The place was similar to the Rothschild Museum in Frankfurt, a mausoleum, it's best possessions also in London, safe from Germankind.

Anyway — pardon my asking — are you sure the guy I met is your father? He was plump, dark, half your size, and talked alot about the fine limp golden hair you had as a little girl. I told him, I didn't know you as a blond. I also didn't show him your photograph.

Curiously he didn't show me any family pics either. How come?

Your lover, André

Dear André,

I am mad at you still. How can you speak 'off the cuff', when
you wear none? You are despicable. We are polite here. We have
etiquette. If we're rude to each other it is because we obey the
rules of rudeness first. We are also clean about ourselves.

My father said, that instead of changing into fresh clothes,
you wore your sweatshirt inside out, teddy bear style, to show
the nubby unstained side. He used to say about the Turkish
vice-consul, 'His left hand is the one with the thumb in the
middle'. I cringe to think that he might say that of you. He
did not. He was kind. He only said that you were smart in
Russian ways, but your arrogance irritated him. It is obvious.

Please, dress, eat and drink well. Allow your opinions only
to entertain, and you will succeed, at least at dinners. Stop
resisting us! Do you wish to lose me?

I hope you were not as bad also, in my father's home as in
mine. I have never lived with a man before, but I still have
happy expectations. Yet you must leave crumbs everywhere.
You look like a caveman in the morning. Are all men this way?
I do not believe it. Nor am I convinced that you must be
Germanic to be a mensch. Though I will admit, I never saw
a dustball till I was eighteen. My mother was very proper.

I do not understand you. Am I not supposed to? In San
Francisco your store was inviting, neat and tidy. You built
cameras to photograph each other, as works of art, or you saw
them as fine furniture, so perfect that no sitter could measure
up. Yes, yes, you did. Are you only perverse then? Must you be?
You are here now. You are with us. You will become one of us.
Can't you see us for our potential? What do your better lenses
hold? Have you the will by us, the courage also, to let me see
what you see? Don't you understand, please, that your quest
is my quest, not for a camera but for the vision, to beautify the
tears in my life, to repair my parents divorce, to redeem my

sense of decay, and my past indifference to my physical self.
You can make me anew. You have done this with your love.
Do it now to last, boldly, yes, yes, on silver photographic paper,
with the sight you gain here.

Please understand, my father again would offer his past to
insure my future. And I will give it back to him. I can if you
help to restore our dreams, to remove our cloud cover, if you
see our possibilities and great accomplishments. Give us good
visions of ourselves. Erase our bitterness. Recreate us as we
formerly were. Then you will find your rare and special
cameras. We will aid you. We need your strange piercing eyes,
to smile in approval. Please, help us win the world, yes, yes,
so that we may win ourselves. We can not do it alone. History
has taught us that.

Do you understand now? Teach us, or we will teach you!
Redeem yourself! Your crumbs will be forgiven.

What is happening to our romance? Sometime you are
wonderful. Other times I hope will not repeat. Can't you stop
being so badly American? You will not lose your freedom here.
Freedom is work, and work makes you free. That is true. You
will obey, or I will not obey you.

Must I always be mad at you? Did you really tell my father
that my dumplings fell flat? And that I am not blond? I am
blond, a subtle blond. My hair is half as dark as yours.

Please, do not feel that, because we criticize you, you have
to out-criticize us. Europeans are simply more critical. We have
the right to be. Our standards are different. But from now on,
I will ask your pardon in advance, so that I do not insult you.
Are you picking up your mail and sticking to your itinerary?

Why do you only photograph me in bed?

Your love, in adversity, Sara

Dear Sara,

It's true. Definitely. Americans are brash, curious creatures, because we want to have greener cabbage, lively breads and every variety of lowfatliving. Food here sucks. Yeah, I could cut my hair, fashion a brush mustache, and join the smoking Euro-masses, but would you recognize me? Would you want to?

I doubt it.

Meanwhile, back in your border reality, the Mercedes took me into East Germany without a visa. To get out I had to empty my pocket of West Mark.

I failed completely on the Polish map. The Mercedes offered no disguise. I tried anyway. I even shaved with sour cream — nothing else presented itself — but the border guards insisted on the right papers, period. I told the sentries, that my consulate said I'd be granted a visa on entry. The youngest guard went giddy on me. "They lie!" he said, laughing. He got in, behind the wheel, drove me 50 yards into Poland, u-turned, and returned me to the exit gate "Now, you will say, you went to Poland. Five dollars please." I paid him in East Mark.

So, you expect me to pay, to play by your rules too? Are they inborn, enshrined somewhere, learned on the street? In Vienna I saw lines of little girls, coins in hand, waiting dutifully for a turn at a curbside amusement ride — a ring of teacup chairs circling a tall white coffee-pot with a curving spout.

It was charming, but as a kid I rode toy rockets, whipping snakes and racing cars. I also saved the torn tickets, in order to paste them together for a second turn. Now I travel in clover-leaves, without luck, and think that I'm lost, at least here.

Sorry to say — whatever I see — I can't help you, or any-one. My search is fruitless. The few common cameras still around are sightless and absurdly expensive. In West Berlin

I came upon a clouded normal Leica lens from the Thirties,
worth $50 at best in the U.S. The guy wanted $400. Yeah, sure.
I protested. "But it's an original," he said, insulted. I told him
I'd sell him 4 for that price. He shrunk back in frustrated anger.
Definitely, Central Europe's tunnel vision stunts everyone else,
when it can.

Perhaps in fact the better items were removed to Russia but
the USSR is impenetrable still, in spite of changes. I can't get a
visa to travel freely, anonymously, on my own. I tried a few
tricks. But forged entry papers and the Russian army hat, that
you gave me, got me shot at, 20 miles in, coming from
Hungary. Two bullets pierced the front fender. I fled. Next
time I'll arm myself also, with a hijacker's attitude.

Still, I've far more in my pockets than I left with. I sold my
Nikon F2 to a Russian border guard. You should've heard
me go on about the camera, "It was made during an age of
optimism, at the beginning of space flight. It's a classic. Look
at the form, the grip, the detailing. You can hold it sweating in
the tropics, anywhere and it won't slip." I got a small fortune,
plus the doctored visa, but that only brought me into rifle
range of the next free-lance bandit.

By the way I had a little accident with the car, no harm,
of no consequence. In Munich, after I picked up your last letter
I backed into a new BMW that'd wedged me into a parking
spot. The people on the street immediately informed on me.
When the car's owner saw no damage, he shrugged. The crowd
was angry with him for not condemning me, regardless.

Also, in East Germany I backed the Mercedes into a tiny
local car, a Trebbie, and smashed its white plastic license plate.
No one complained. Not a word.

So it goes. In spite of your latest impossible demands, I'd

still rather be with you, sharing the chemistry of your kitchen, your *Runkelrube Suppe,* fennel salad, and your personal dumplings, even if it means I have to develop my film in the grim dark of a starless night world.

Maybe we happened too fast. Then again, all Russians are big baby bears, I hear.

My rudeness is just self-preservation, you realize, I hope.

Your blinded lover-on-the-loose,
André

p.s.

If you want more news, check the newspapers. Each is blind-ered by a different perspective, but all are available at the railroad station. Nazi, Jewish, communist, etc. stack nicely on the same rack. By the way, some of the wanted faces on the post office wall are familiar. I met them briefly at the culture club in San Francisco. They asked my assistance in seeing great distances. I thought that they, unlike you, wanted to see far into the future. But they didn't have any money, even for the materials, so I didn't help. Should I check on rewards?

Wow! Your silence is telling. You're seriously mad.

Okay, sure, I'd love to expose you to the best of your culture, and fly you up on its hypnotic wings — to the threatening expressionist films of the 1920s, *Dr. Mabuse, Metropolis,* and *The Cabinet of Caligari* — or to the enthrall of the 1820's and Beethoven's sublime trials, but Germany is rebuilding a different past, of smug brick, Sunday soup and vaginal inspection. West German women suspected of having an abortion outside the country are internally examined on return, without consent, and on the evidence arrested. Are you aware of that, *Frau* Feminist?

I'm learning. People tell me about themselves. I witness things inadvertently. I still don't see, in the now, what you want me to, whatever the camera at hand.

Why don't you come with me? I'll keep looking, but how can I trade, even with the electronically embedded plastic of the new, for the dense cherrywood of another time, when it's gone. War destroys entirely, you know, or am I wrong?.

Seriously, take a month off, tour the East with me, show me the way, and to your lost treasures.

Were they stashed in Poland by chance? At the RR station I heard that the Poles are only Slavic Germans, whose anthem, commonly sung in school, celebrates the day when their flag will fly over the Ukraine again.

Hey! Is your stolen past in Russia? I'd try again myself, through Finland, but can't afford the hotel bill, paid in advance, for a visa. In any case, is there a best of Austria to hide? Just what promising metal is your lab engineering, my dear? The invisible kind, for stealth?

Tell your father to hurry meanwhile and buy what ever he can, due east of the Berlin wall. Physics professors

there just sold their research institute to a Swiss hotel corp.
Seemingly they were only professors of Marxist-Leninism
to begin with, i.e., party hacks, quick to capitalize on their
country's collapse. Everything's up for sale, except some apples
left to rot on the trees. Small birds pick at them through the
winter frost. Communist fruit isn't too tasty, it seems.

You see, I can find opportunities in the East, but not the
right ones for you or us. Anyway, the small windows of
corrupt opportunity won't last, but the ozone economy will.
Manufacturing is moving in quickly.

I am photographing though. Our car, as well as the ruins,
still show their bullet holes. Missionaries crawl all over the
place, like maggots. Polaroid film is everywhere, for Western
tourists. Yet people are fleeing even faster. It's impossible for
anyone from an East Bloc country, or even from West Germany
now, to get a visa to the U.S., unless he or she buys a return
ticket.

But nothing's changing really. It's mostly a matter of
tourism and shopping opportunities. The children in the
East appear tired of waving in welcome to an endless line of
Mercedes, VWs, BMWs, while their fathers push a plow behind
a horse, reliving the 17th century.

Whatever the time, in both Germanies, the natural species
have shrivelled. Everywhere there are just scavenger crows,
mice, wasps, and dour people. The imperial eagle flies only on
the flag, it's a caricature of itself, medieval, without authority,
but everyone believes in it anyway. You can't really expect me
to also!

Today I saw a true German, in a fine dark overcoat, pick up
a parking ticket from a puddle, to find which car it belonged
on. I left before his diligence led to me.

And yesterday at a West post office, a teacher on a day trip
circled the lobby, reading the rules word for word to her 8 year

old students, as they hurried after her, dropping their gloves, tripping over themselves, in an effort to keep up with her relentless enthusiasm for the directions over the mail drop, the prescripts of the telegraph clerk, the signs over the banking window, and the protocol for telephone callers, as well as the laws of the lobby itself.

Meanwhile playground bullies are encouraged. Last night I watched some tougher teenagers playing *führer* to the full moon. In the name of "Right of Way", they'll grow easily into road killers, with their parents still watching. Scary!

I can't and don't want to see what's lost or how finding it would help us.

I should send for my tools, and make cameras again — there's need for a new warp to reality here — but I'm not in a position, like the government, to lend people the money, that I print, to buy from me, and then quota the sale into being.

Oh well, better luck next life, huh? My camera eyes are getting well worn in this one, though. Can I come back now? There's nothing else to report, except that I enjoy the bone-piercing cold, and the raw wind of the moment. Hopeless, aren't I? The coal dust in the air makes for beautiful sunsets. That's why.

By chance, is it the Hapsburgs you want reborn?

As it turns out, I have a job now, of the shadow variety, but it's a job nonetheless, keeping my country abreast of the cultural melt and the sperm traffic, so to speak.

Your love, in eternal perversity,
André

Dear André,

Be harsh, wit as you will, but I want you to know, I am going in circles about us, and having many bad thoughts. Since you have been here, we have not been getting along, as you are well aware. Are you not? I still love you as much, but I have come out of the trance you kept me in, and now I am confused, as never before. You should not have come. You are so different suddenly, lackadaisical in your personal habits, and useless in your professional life. You do not hang up your coat (a couch is not a closet). You waste resources (every cut of paper napkin counts). You leave the bathroom towel wet (I flick the water off me before I dry myself). You are no help to my science (you have not been lately), and you refuse to share my hopes and dreams (you are impossibly prejudiced). What else is wrong with you? I expect you to confess to your flaws, or you will never correct them, if you can.

Atsch! Ech...I am becoming German myself, critical and philosophical and pointless. I need your purpose, whatever way you are...yes, yes, I do, yet the price is too high. Still you are my marching music in the morning as well as the whirling-center of my night. Without you, I can not dream or wake up.

What started my circling, though, was a clipping my father sent from the Vienna newspaper, an ad saying "Diplomats Needed." The ad was only for a school for diplomats, but it renewed my earliest ambition. Scientists in government circles are well-respected. People would have to listen to me. Can you see me as the Consul to China? Like Austria, China is an imperial bureaucracy, though no one admits that. Vienna was built to be the capitol of an empire. Yes, yes, if you must know, being Austrian is important to me. I did not think how much until I returned. I can no longer deny it or hide it. I dislike your criticism of German culture. To a point it is okay, I agree, but it is my culture also, and criticizing it is denying me. The war ended long ago, though I know Austria does not seem to think so. But Germany lost ten million people. That is too many by any measure. Do you think it not enough? Would you count eye for eye?

Oh, I do not know what to think. You would derail my career. I may need to travel to anywhere in the world at any moment, to represent my country with scientific rightness. I am a bureaucrat at heart, I have discovered, and am not ashamed to admit it. It is a virtue. Analyzing astro-molecular order is equally prized, I believe —

Oh, I can not think straight when I think of you. Please continue your search, or whatever you are doing. Give me time to sort out my thoughts.

Worse to worse, at least bring back postcards. I collect them, like my father his stamps. Whenever I go places myself, usually I buy the postcards first, so that I know what to see. You are visiting many scenes before my chance.

I wish that I were free to show you my country, but that is not possible now. My experiments are in progress again and producing awful unwanted results. It must be your bad wishes.

You must go on your own. Do you think no postcards exist of the images, of the life that I want? I could make them myself, if you would help. The brass lens you sold me still warps every-thing, you know. The distortion is very incredible. You said, that you can make any lens do anything. just as you can process any film in any developer. I do not believe you. You sales-pitched me too. Your lens is limited. You are also, but you worked on me. Perhaps you preserved my youth in pictures, but why can you not make Europe look as real, as it is to me, not in another time, but now? The past is still here, in front of us. The lens should merely highlight it. Why does it not? Instead, when I use it, the lens shades us harshly. This is not the purpose it was made for. You have done something to it. Admit to it.

I have to sleep now. The new flash lamp in my lab buzzes so loud it tires me. The high energy UV pulsing requires my energy as well it seems, but I must be strong, stronger than my machines, to master them.

I am gathering family pictures to show you. I look my best in my baby album.

Incidentally, Nili says hello, via e-mail. She landed a good position with NASA and wants to hear from you. With her husband running your store, it is successful again. You should have made sure that he failed. Just the thought of him makes me shiver. He is a bloated insect, and nothing else!

Did you say that you are now working? I do not believe it, because I am your job, and you are not performing. When was the last time you kissed my belly button? Do I have the right to ask?

Did you really see a woman strip-searched? Where?

Lovingly,
Sara

Dear Sara,

I hope you're not serious. You, a diplomat? You'll start a war. Did Hitler also think he was blond? I'm beginning to understand why the *Führer* had to be half-Austrian. Is this where your feminism is leading?

Dear *Frau Doktor,* you don't need a camera or a postcard view, new or old. You need an altered mind-set. And your country needs a true revolution, starting with a change in name and language. As *Ôsterreich,* the East Reich, it will persevere, sure, but only to its provincial limit.

Am I supposed to be your Berta Riefenstahl, bitch innocent and propagandist, with a funnel-vision view of your cause?

And what's this about traveling? You hide underground wherever you are, whenever you can. Why not do it in the U.S. then? In Los Alamos, you could hang out in a basement lab on top of an aspen mountain at least. And I could search for a vision myself, or be a watcher on the ramparts, or craft new lenses, in the Siberia of my time, the landscapes of the Southwest.

Reconsider, my love. Don't make a mistake you'll regret.

Yes, I know your country's trying to join the E.C. and may want someone to lead it from its autocratic past, but can anyone, even for appearance sake?

You need more immediate persuasion. Definitely!

Soon my dear,
André

"Hi Sara! I'm sorry, I didn't mean to be mean, in my last letter."

"We have to talk, now, before you come back. Your attitude is so awful."

"I'm only learning."

"I do not know you anymore."

"You know everything you need to."

"Yes, yes, you are great in bed. Otherwise you are terrible. Are you the same with every woman?"

"If I'm being American —"

"You do not deny it. Huhu. This is terrible. I have not been this close with someone in so long —"

"We could stay in bed all the time."

"You would get bored."

"You'd get pregnant."

"I do not want to be."

"Well, that makes things interesting."

"I am afraid, you will change your mind."

"Don't be, why should I?"

"For 20 reasons, or no reason at all."

"True...Are you crying? I hear tears."

"Yes, I do not know why. Is it epidemic? I have nothing more to be depressed about than usual. You can be so nice. I am not used to niceness. You have to be strict with me but not mean."

"No thanks. I'd have to be strict with myself then."

"What about birth control? Why will you not use condoms? The lubricated ones smell bad but I like them."

"I can wear them once in awhile. They're half as good as nothing."

"You are so terrible. Are you circumcised?"

"Don't you know."

"I never looked."

"Not even when —"

"I am very shy. I would not know anyway."

"Are your eyes closed in the lab too? How are the little molecules?"

"Misbehaving."

"Do they ever behave?"

"Oh yes, they can be very cute."

"What's wrong with me then?"

"You are a dream, a fairy tale."

"You mean I don't get to come true?"

"Yes. No. I don't know. I accept whatever happens, but I need a safety zone. Come back anyway. If you do not, we will be unfinished, always. I bought Russian chocolates for you, in gold paper. They are delicious. You can have all you want. Nili suggested it. She said in her letter, 'Enjoy yourself, you lunatic!' No one ever called me that before. I guess, if I am not pregnant yet, I am not going to be."

"See you next week. By the way I thought Germany only lost five million people in the war."

"When I'm arguing it's ten. Hurry back...I love you...I can not wait to look into your eyes again...If only I could see what they do...André, are you there?"

Dear André,

Every time you call, you throw me off the little bit of balance I have. Even three minutes on the phone strikes like thunder. This must stop. You just hung up but it seems like our conversation needs to continue. There is so much to say. Can I speak the truth?

Sitting down to write this letter, I realize again why it is so hard for me to reveal my hopes and my goals. You are trying to control me. You are my control. Perhaps I need control. But you have overpowered me, with insult and indifference and love. Why can I not dominate you instead? Do not Europeans have the critical edge over Americans anymore?

I went to Hameln yesterday. I do not know why I went, perhaps because there are mice in the apartment. They are shredding the refrigerator insulation for a nest. Can you do something about them? You are my pied piper. Will you also steal my childhood from me, as well as my molecules? What is your fee for leaving? How much do I owe you? I look into your dark round eyes and never know what is developing. I see love, mirrors, death —

I am losing it again. I can not help it. Maybe it is biological. I am learning things about myself that I did not want to know. But I must be honest with myself — Ech! Now I sound American.

I need to become drunk. I do not know what I need. I need you.

Love,
Sara

Bad news. Return immediately. I am pregnant. I cried for an hour when I found out. My life is over. My mother was furious with me, because you are a foreigner. She is afraid that she will be left alone.

I want to have an abortion anyway. I will need the approval of two doctors, in a different district. You must take me. I have no one else.

I feel terrible. I am sick and the birds wake me earlier every morning. Do they not have anything better to do? Is this their sole purpose in life? I long for my mother's vacuum cleaner. It always soothed me to sleep. Should I send for her?

I do not want to. I reread your letter last night, the one from Vienna after your visit to my father. For your information, my country does not believe in Freud and never did. But our ministers believe in American tourist dollars, and like to see foreigners paying for our souvenir money. Freud was anti-women, as my father is, in his flirtations. Are you going to be like him always?

I also played with teacups as a child, yes, yes, but I had a toy village too, and its mayor wrote letters to other mayors who answered me with polite grace, and invited me to balls, which you have never done. Will you ever? Where are you? Do I have to come to get you?

"So it's abortion time in the fatherland, is it?"

"I go in circles but always return to the same point."

"Will the doctors consent?"

"When I tell them who the father is."

"Really? It's that simple? Then what's with your mother?

"She sent me pills."

"And?

"I thought about taking them, but the thought did not stick."

"Do I have anything to say?

"It is my decision."

"I'm irrelevant."

"If you were, I would already have seen the doctors. That is what I want to do though. I can make an appointment tomorrow. Will you be back to take me?"

"I'm 600 miles away. You're asking alot."

"Only what I deserve. Come back, I will not decide anything for certain until you are here."

"I'm not close enough?"

"No. Have you not learned? What have you learned? Tell me the difference between Austrians and Germans?"

"Each thinks she's better than the other. Even your father said that Austria is only a second cousin in importance to Germany, after Switzerland. Do the Swiss think that way?"

"So, so. What do you think?"

"I haven't been to Switzerland."

"No, about us, the baby we would have."

"Where would it be born?"

"Here. I can not interrupt my experiments. Do not

worry. To be born here means nothing. You must show your grandmother's birth certificate, and if it is not German, you are denied benefits, everything. The baby would be Austrian, unless we got married, then I do not know what it would be…but I am inclined to have an abortion. I want to travel. I have always traveled."

"But you're not traveling. When you get to where you're going, you live underground, under mercury vapor lamps, with exotic complex electronic eyes to let you see, in an effort to discover the secrets of —"

"— science, yes, yes, but you could help me come outside. I have been asking you to."

"Did you get my letter about Los Alamos?"

"Yes, bada bada, you want me to work in a bomb factory?"

"Other things are done there. Besides which, they wouldn't let you near the bombs. You're not American."

"I would have to become one, to work there."

"Not necessarily. Would you let the baby be?"

"A citizen? No."

"What're we going to do?"

"I do not know. We are in trouble, are we not?"

"How pregnant are you?"

"Six weeks, six days, ten-and-a-half hours, I believe. The medical report suggests that I conceived the night before you left for Poland. My phone bill came today also. I owe 627 Mark. Talking to you in the U.S. cost 23 *pfenning* for each 4.42 seconds."

"We could fly back."

"Never, never, never! I will not kill my mother and be on Freud's couch forever!"

Terminal Name - 6000000021, $CONSOLE - 31000000036
Connection $A created.

* * * W A R N I N G * * *

You have accessed a United States Government computer.
Use of this computer without authorization or for purposes
for which authorization has not been extended is a violation
of Federal law (99-474).

psword: Night Scope $shell: bin/arc/NASA/gov
time: 20:03:10 CET action: reaction: unknown
subject: Hi! return path: Amconsul London

Hello Nili,

Sara's a surprise, always. She shouldn't be. In ways, she's as
predictable as her culture, as mapped as a periodic table. Here,
she counts everything. Apart from me, her life is numbers,
as if she's suddenly rediscovered them. They're more important
to her than what they stand for. She can tell you how many
wooden matches I use each day to light our cranky stove,
how many pico-seconds her newest metal will last before it
explodes, how many convertible cars of this or that kind we've
passed on the road. But it isn't a childhood game. It's proof
against the world. She argues for numeric repeatability, into
ordering the minutiae of the day. I insist that numbers don't
count. Even in the lab improvisation is everything. She doesn't
agree. She goes through my garbage, with a calculator mind-
set, charting my wastes. She, like her country, wants to be the
measure of all things. Still she's a scientist, forgetful about herself. As you sometimes can't remember your phone listing, she
can't keep the days of her period straight. Yes, she's pregnant.
 We went for an abortion, twice, each time to Kassel. The

abortion clinic is down the block from a children's toy store, on a wide cobblestone street. The first time, a tank, speeding ahead of us, rammed a BMW, and totaled it, blocking the *autobahn.* The tank was new, had all its cannons in place, and *"Fahrschule,"* driving school, painted on the turret.

On our second try, the exhaust of another tank cooked some paint off Sara's Mercedes, but we arrived on schedule. I left Sara, pale and nervous, in with the doctor. His nurse told me to come back in precisely 2 hours. I wandered the main street. Looking in the toy store nearby pained me too deeply. Much of the time I stood in front of an unpretentious pet shop feeling as bleak, wilted and sickly as the window display. After an idle hour, I took my car for a restless ride around town. I saw nothing, I couldn't see. But I began to realize how much having a family might mean to me. Returning, I pulled into the last free parking spot at the clinic, just in front of another car, driven by a stuffed pork-sausage type with a vegetable-brush mustache. The guy went into fits. He leaped out, screaming at me. How dare I block a public road, to keep him from his space! I answered him in English, saying that I'd arrived first, legitimately, and he could fuck off. He screamed, in German, "Speak German in Germany!" I said, you understand me. He stuttered, in English, perhaps the only 2 words that he knew: "G-go home!" "You go home!" I said. That did it. He gagged on his rage, slapped his hands to his side and left redly, in frustration. I'd thwarted his belligerence but it was contagious. I wanted to rush into the clinic, pull Sara out of the doctor's grasp and crunch the man's head with his forceps, or suction his brains into the vacuum apparatus. I might have but thought it was too late. So, instead, I went meekly inside, just in time to meet Sara coming out of his office. Solicitously I reached to support her. But she stood erect, cheerful, with color in her cheeks. "Are you all right?" I asked. "I did not do it!" she said proudly, happily. I hugged her, told her I loved her and asked what she'd done for 2 hours. "I talked to the doctor," she said, "in a way that I can not with you or my mother." We rode home in silence. I pressed for details, but all she'd say was, nothing's changed. She's acting as if her life's no different in the least. She refuses to tell her boss that she's pregnant.

We won't get her back to the U.S. easily, if at all, though she knows her talent is wasted here. Comparatively, the science is often second rate. Most accomplishments come from pig-headed pursuit of a small object. Many a lifetime is spent gathering one set of data and endlessly reinterpreting it. Sara's aware of this. It's possible that the baby may well make a difference, but not yet. I can't convince her of anything. Foreigners in the U.S. usually lose their foreignness but she's regained hers. If she does return to San Fran, she may crawl out from under the weight of her history again and stand naked in the street once more, anxious to cloth and reclothe herself with newness and invention, as we might, but I can't be sure. I'm losing all sense of definition.

I hope the baby's normal. Sara's in the lab all the time. Between her work and mine, any combination of horror is possible. The electro-magnetic radiation that surrounds her is intense. An unseen laser beam could burn a hole clean through her. The danger is quite real, she thinks it's remote. At least she quit smoking.

I'm contaminated also. Before I left S.F., I found at Macy's downtown, after a day in the darkroom, that a high alcohol essence whitened my hands, removing the Victoria Green dye mordanted into my skin by a selenium toner. I sampled the spray while searching for a present to bring Sara. (Clorox and ferrocyanide didn't work as well.) My genes must be jumping.

Sara doesn't care, but I'm afraid she will be upset that I'm writing to you, whatever she suspects, but I need your help, to stay here. I can't be just an itinerant vigilant.

My exotic cameras aren't creating contacts anyway. Ordinary Ricohs and Konicas are the affordable peak of pride. The general public has no peripheral awareness of the professional field. Most people don't know what a Leica is, let alone that it was made here and that I can use it from waist level. I've written to my former U.S. clients but no commissions resulted. Our national agencies, while offering small tasks, seem to want me to test the future by myself.

I finally did cross into Russia, hoping to root out my family past, only to find that I'm from San Francisco after all. Everywhere else is foreign to me when I'm alone, it seems.

My only other discovery is that Germany's divorcing us to remarry itself, and sanctify its bulge. That's right, German is a religion, and Naziism its fundamentalism. Scolding scapegoating bureaucrats are everywhere, like clerics. They grow disembodied voices, to let you know how unimportant you are. Indeed they hide your life from you, absorbing your every detail, leaving you aware of their rules only. Am I being paranoid? No. We, Sara and I, are on our own. And I am a ghost. Someone like Odo, Sara's cousin, accepts the robes of the state over his life. He isn't aware of his own sullen silence. Germany speaks to him, through him, ceaselessly. The undying bureaucracy continues to bloat, surviving all wars, erupting in them, managing them, regardless of the political party in charge or style of power. My aunt sent me a 1905 British guide to Germany. It could've been written in 1942. The people here bitterly worship themselves still. Spiteful control prevails, but everyone bows to the bureaucracy, and obeys regardless, yet the more they do, the more they expect the rest of the world to obey them. They can make themselves strangers anywhere. Definitely.

Nevertheless, they need us to carry the cost — to sanction

their incest with unending cash praise. Keep up the imports, thank you kindly, U.S., we'll pay you back with German lessons.

Unfortunately, Sara's no exception to her culture now. She's reconciled to it. She's been wearing flag-yellow blouses, with broken red & black stripes. She knows though, you must pay with numbers for every number you get from the state. Information isn't free, only instruction is. She's as taxing as the new Germany will be on itself. I can't do anything for her or about her for the moment.

But I'm pretty sure, I can acquire a stash of Polish amber, for your husband, yes, petrified goo, buggy sap, but there'll be no coded messages inside, in spite of appearances. The store could sell these as novelties or jewels, natural, ancient, essence of life shit, and hint at other secrets, that I've yet to find.

I'll be happy to leave here. Sara — *Frau* Heavy Metal, as her group calls her — wants me for something, but it isn't a baby. Fatherhood is a concept she respects but not in any other language. She'd like to prove herself better than her own father, of that I'm certain. Perhaps there's some pact between her and her mother. I'm not sure, but another dimension is operating. Definitely her father is a hole in the ground. Something is buried with him, calling out, echoing into his voice, disrupting his poise. Yet he seems too good-natured, too contained to act destructively. He's like the lake Sara told me about, glaringly calm, with a Messerschmidt mine underneath.

I should be in Russia really, and make it my mission. The science there is superb, and the turmoil an opportunity. I've made an effort to meet the Russians here, that have been wooed to study at Sara's Institute, and will report on them later.

By the way, Sara's father told me why he's so tolerant of the U.S. At the end of WW2, the Russians advancing on Vienna wanted to coach the U.S. on how to "handle a conquered people", but the U.S. refused to take lessons and forced the Russians to retreat a bit.

Congratulations to you and your husband for your varied successes. If possible, send some inspiration, and a few of my boxes from storage, one marked "Tools" and the other "In Progress". I may soon have a baby to support, or a monster to bury. Perhaps you can get the crates here before I head for London. I'm going to dig in my aunt's backyard as well, before the birth, to learn more of my own past.

Kindly be discreet in talking to Sara. Give her the benefit of the doubt and the baby a chance also. Things will happen as they should, hopefully, for all of us.

Find out also, if I should bring a few Russians home. Tell the Washington vacuum, it's possible. Or would that be adding to our national problems? I understand that a third of our doctoral graduates, in chemistry at least, are already foreign born. Makes me wonder, are our labs so inspiring, or is shuttle science now the way of the world?

Sara likes me to come and go, so I'll continue to explore on the road, even if I'm only finding pot-hole repairs.

Yours,
Agent André,
on Satellite Patrol

"Hi Sara, does your mother know, that you're still pregnant?"

"I am sorry, André, I forgot to tell her."

"How could you forget?"

"I will tell her, right after the election."

"The baby'll be born by then."

"And everything changed, forever, I'm afraid."

"Nothing's different. I'm carrying the baby's sonogram in my wallet, but you're still in the lab and —"

"You are unemployed. Say it. How are you going to support us?"

"Like your mice, by shredding plastic bags. Recycling, it's called. Or I could risk —"

"No! We are not living between refrigerator walls! Is it too late? Should I call the doctor again?"

"If we've made a mistake."

"Do you think so? I hope not. I can not know, can I? Do you believe what you told Frowin?"

"You didn't have to introduce us —"

"He is your relation now."

"Not by blood, not till we're married. Even then —"

"How could you call the Greens the Garbage Gestapo?"

"That's what they are. They just want the authority, to police their parents."

"Frowin believed you. And when you said, 'German's the language of the Nazis,' in front of the visiting Russians, he was crushed."

"I didn't expect him to be. Why was he?"

"He is seduced by your cameras. You speak well. You see now. And he trusts your knowledge of optics, more than he appreciates mine."

"His mistake. Your scale's astronomical. You understand the need for gravitational lensing, to see, to weigh the dark matter of the universe. Frowin's a fool."

"So, so! That is how you think of Germany? As dark matter, not to be seen. Is it? It is, is it not? But I have found my country again and, my love, I have stolen your sperm. No matter what my biology tells me to do, I will not give up again. You will always be mine now, even if you and Chlorine had an affair. Miss Molecute —"

"Nili?"

"She did not get pregnant. I did. You will take a new life. You can not sell anything to us. You will see our truth. We have Leitz. We do not need plastic beads."

"Sorry, dearie. Throwaways are here to stay. Besides which, the British and Swiss own Leica."

"But it is the pride of Germany!"

"The company went on the block. It lost too much money. But the English and Swiss are doing well with it."

"Because the British had so many colonies."

"Maybe, but they've learned, arrogant bullies make bad salesmen. Your people only learned the mirror lesson. The British sense of fair play works well for them now. Your father's stamp collection shows —"

"— nothing. Ask to see his glass plates — Oh my god! What did I say! Please, sell yourself wherever you have to, but stay away. You can not come back now. Just be here for the birth. I will take care of myself in this meantime. It will be best."

"Sara, what're you telling —"

"I am hanging up! Do not come back. I will not answer the door bell!"

Dear Sara,

Hello from Assisi. I called your father for a handle on you. He invited me to meet him here, and bring you. I brought 2 of the Russians from your lab instead, for an international confab in Verona. Actually I'm still waiting for your old man to show. Meanwhile, it's enchanting here, with fog & fig coffee, lace baby bibs & innocenti (small Fiats). No sacred silence in fact but the plate of gesture is full. I could get into the habit of Italy, but there aren't enough lifetimes. Verona was 10,000 Juliets. One said, "We talk hands and we talk feet, but we don't speak much English here." How different you'd be if you were born this far south! Of course, Romeo & Juliet died before their life together began. Your father said on the phone, that your mother still thinks Italy is a small town in Austria. Obliging you, I'll stay.

Love — your André

Dear Sara,

Hello again. I'm still in Assisi, still waiting for your father, but surrounded now by corn spaghetti and holy thimbles, nuns at the bar, a monk in Birkenstocks racing his motor scooter, with a flat of mushrooms on the floor board. The hocus-pocus of Catholicism is everywhere, all stores selling medievalism — mace & chains, Madonnas, swords & sanctimoniousness. Meanwhile a cat left a freshly cut fishhead under my car hood. Bees like to eat the highway dead from my radiator. I'm also waiting for an old woman, bent over a broom that's swept a thousand floors, to unblock my way. I plan to cool off, at the *"zona peep,"* the view turn-out, at the lake near Perugia. I had hoped to fill myself with home again. Assisi is a sister city to San Francisco, ridiculously. Strange pilgrimage I'm on. Now I suspect, your father won't show. What'll we name the baby?

André, your lover

Dear Sara,
Your father invited me, for a week in Austria, by way of
apology, for being unable to meet me. It seems his new wife
had her own code-red emergency. He didn't volunteer and I
didn't ask for details. I think he wanted to give me his blessings,
in a "holy place", but his new wife isn't the virgin she used to
be. Or maybe he wanted us to have a double wedding. He
married his nurse, you know, last week.

I left the Russians behind in good hands and tunneled
north. A cloud like a squid ate the mountain top. Thick
tentacles of fog held the pass open. The sunset is beautiful.
You are here, my love.
André

Dear Sara,
It's Vienna again. The Hunderwasser house, the strudel steps,
the subway rips. I tried another visit to Freud, and watched the
images on the wall, with text in hand this time. The living book
let me in, between its covers. Am I going crazy? Right now
coffee is being served at a cafe with crocheted table cloths.

Your father is here too and happy that the low winter sky
is lifting, and that the dismal mood of Vienna may soon disappear. He even promised to give me his glass-plate collection
of photographs, after the baby is born, but he won't reveal
more about them yet. Meanwhile, he honored me with an
Austrian calendar. It has days for banking saints, a Saint
Adolph, and even a Saint Sara, patron of the gypsies. Your
father wants to choose his grandchild's name, and decide our
"touristic possibilities." I told him we were converting.
Your lover, with sperm ever waiting,
André

"André, *hallo* my love. Thanks for the postcards. Italy is very Italian, is it not? Do you still think, Austrians are only grim Germans? Even so, please do not take my father seriously or accept any presents from him. You must ignore him, for me. And do not go anywhere that you should not. We have enough trouble. My mother calls every day now. She said, that it was all right to bring home a souvenir from America, meaning you, but not to let him take over the house. She must be talking to my father, but will not admit it. I said, I have sent you traveling again. She wants you to call and ask permission for me, even while I am quite pregnant and showing. Do what you want. I have decided not to fight with you anymore, even if you steal our Russians. By the by, a letter from Hamburg says that your cargo has arrived. Nili is quick when it counts. But come home first. I want you here."

"I am here."

"Next to me."

"Can't we have the baby in the U.S?"

"No, I have my reasons, I am selfish too, I admit it."

"By being selfish, do you get what you want?"

"Not always. But we must not discuss politics now."

"I won't be the shadow to your selfishness."

"I need you to be. Why do you like me if you will not accept me?"

"I've always given you a hard time. You didn't mind till you retrenched here. Your world would straight-jacket me, if I —"

"Just stop on your way then, before you pick up your toys. And please, leave your umbrella outside, if it's raining. I will make my grandmother's gooseberry jam. And I want many more postcards, yes, like those from Italy."

Dear Sara,

Here I am again, in Hamburg now, still on Central European time, eating dead woman's jam, breaking apart shipping crates by hand, and waiting with the drunk truckers to pay the port my alien surcharge. Outside, crossing the harbor, the wishbone suspension bridge welcomes the ice wind and Nicaraguan bananas, ginger without sugar, and clothesracks of arriving calendars, into my freezing eyes. Strange, the time warp I've traveled. I went from summer in Italy to winter in Germany in 2 days. But soon I'll be racing away from the North Sea, shouting above the howling of our pack mule Mercedes, joyful, expectant, returning to sweet bakeries on every corner and an angry mistress in command mode, pregnant with new life....Rumania happened today. The collapse of central authority at the turn of the decade continues, more quickly than the *autobahn* allows. Definitely! Still, the kilometers go by faster than the miles. I love you.

André

Dear Sara,

May have to push the car home. Austria, even Czechoslovakia, are day trips but our mustard mule needs a new starter kick. Not terrible. Life with a laser jockey always needs finer tuning. Are your nipples still swelling to the ready? I've got my tools and a dozen view cameras with me. Should I shoot this lame car and leave it?

The big news from home is that S.F. won the Superbowl again (football, of course).

Your lover,

André

"André, what happened to our Russians? The conference ended weeks ago. No one has heard from them. Their notebooks, programs, results — everything is gone. My *Chef* is furious. Without their data, he has no interpretation, no paper to put his name on. And millions of Marks in equipment are idled. I know you have a secret life, separate from me. What is it?"

"I offered the Russians a democracy primer, an open door to Los Alamos. The boys are waiting for me in the States."

"Very funny! You stay where you are. Where are you? I am leaving the lab now."

"To come along? Should I pack for you? I'm flying out. Have to. I can't sprout eyes for you, or grow roots here. I'm feeling like a kept couch potato. Stranded."

"You have projects, do you not? And good ideas. I liked the chess set in the hinged walnut shell."

"That? I finished the carving last night. It's unsold. What's the difference if I'm gone? You only come home to sleep."

"Is that so? Then leave if you must. I don't need you anymore. The baby will happen without you. You are interfering, with everything, with my entire life!"

"Without even trying."

"You have served your purpose. Leave! I will buy the ticket."

"Can I choose the flight?"

"André, please. Just leave me alone till I tell you to come back. I have secrets too."

"Tell?"

"No. The Russians stole our scientists after the last war, and now you are stealing our Russians. Please stop!"

"When I get my sperm back."

"No. The baby will stay with me, here, but you must go."

Okay Lady,

Keep my sperm, see if I care. I've a few billion more. What's your plan for the baby anyway? You won't get past the *Stadtrat's* net. Go ahead, deny me, tell city hall that I'm your newest experiment. Sorry sir, the flagellum fell off, the test tube slipped, we know no father, the micro-label was lost with the tail.

Is this the latest feminist fad? Why do you want to be a mistress instead of a wife? Yeah, I mean to goad you!

I don't see the point of returning now to the U.S. but I will. Why turn down a free ticket where I'm not wanted? Are you afraid I'll get bored watching your belly grow, or that you'll need my help? Sure, you can take care of yourself, but you will need assistance, like it or not, soon enough. Don't worry, I'm on the plane, on my way, but I'm planning a nest for you in San Francisco, after I check with my aunt and uncle, Sam and Liberty, to see if they've any silver dollars left.

Guess what? I just cleared customs in New York. They waved me through without an inspection. They know there's nothing competitive, worth bringing home from Europe, for an American. Too bad I didn't.

Nevertheless, will you tell me if and when you change your mind, or will you be too proud? How seriously should I take you? You told me last night that I can do whatever I want now, as long as I don't have other children elsewhere. Do you still mean that? Are you pushing your luck or just my buttons?

Remember the nude on my wall, who you identified with? She was so different from you, yet so much the same. She and I had a wonderful affair but a horrible marriage. Luckily it ended quickly and there were no children. I think I know what happened then. I know I don't know what's happening now.

With baffled love,
Your Male Donor

Dear Sara,

Home again where I belong, Drunk again too, on the night
nectars of spring, I crushed the urge to crash a zip code party,
showcasing black lips and slashed nylons, 2 stories up. My feet
are too far away, to make the climb. While ice-white lights frost
San Francisco Bay, the ship windows shine.

Intense dreams of you in love. Stiff and limp at once, I prop
myself up on the dock and find a tasseled pumpkin bookmark
holds my place. Reading unminds my homeless days. The silent
subway tunnels the bay below this parking pier.

André

Dear Sara,

It's the year of the horse, in the lunar calendar. Frightened
awake by firecracker prawns, the subway starts at 6. I walk
the dawn, thinking of you. The wooden sign of the Electric
Laundry dims. The deerhide lance waits in a leathered window.
Sandal traffic hides the bronze inlay, a compass rose.

Now the dragon, sleeping under the street, wakes in silk to
70 hands lifting. The Chinese new year plate is orange sliced,
but mouth-watering marmalade fills the glass glory downtown.
What color's god?

A taxi lefts in front of me, but the full moon, hanging
between street lights, leads me into the broken sky. In the east,
a Golden Pearl burns into sight. Suddenly the moon sets in
surprise as the fog rises. Dreaming, I love you more than my
waking eyes have known.

André

Dear André,

Yet, you still *see* Nili! What type of nuclear waste is her husband? She is on her way to Poland, for him, on your advice. I invited her to stop here. She accepted. She will bring trouble. She is too American. I do not trust her. She asks everything of me but not to know me. What is she telling you that you listen? Her astro-chemistry is fine, but mine may surprise her. I have secret molecules that she can not conceive. Also I applied to work at IBM in Switzerland and at Bell Labs in New Jersey, for next year, after the baby. You will follow me! Nili will land on a moon of Neptune by then, and I will measure her disappointment from here, as if it were a pile of dimes. Yes, yes, she will be a pay toilet of despair when I am through with her. Meanwhile you behave yourself. You have work to do, to earn your future. You are going to be a father, and your chances for fooling around are over. Do you understand?
Sara

Dear André,

I'm losing it again. When I went to my birth class, sitting at the table with ten other expectant mothers, was a black-boned skeleton, in a hooded white robe, who went unmentioned. I told Frowin, I have made a mistake, I will be an awful mother. He said, I will grow into the role. I can not believe. Meanwhile, I'm invited by the Chancellor to a reception for those outlanders like myself who have government grants. I am afraid to go. The baby shows, and if that fat cabbage, the *Führer,* wears black flaps to congratulate me, I will faint. I would throw up the baby in his face if I could, and nail *him* to a billboard instead.

I love you. *Sara*

Cheer up! Listen! My mind's blazing and I'm not drunk.

Today I watched a fire eater, at a street carnival, breathe out a flame like a mushroom cloud flaring back on itself. The searing sight of fire sobered me. All at once I thought I saw the shape of your mind. The velvet folds of flame flowered so redly, they would fix a formula in a frozen eye. Who sees the shape of our future? You? I? Our baby on its sonogram screen?

Imagine the wildest molecule, growing. It exists in you now. Nowhere else. You told me, you hoped for a love child outside of marriage, beyond my control. You have what you wanted. The baby shares your brain. At the same time, she'll suck the calcium out of your bones. She's your uninhibited explosion, still inside.

My breath also is gone without you. Definitely. Even casual love is more real than either of us. It leads where we can't go. Can you see its refocusing shape? Then let it flower out to me calmly. It'll make all the difference to know, to see, to taste, to unfold with you, however surreally. My bones hurt for you. Why're you still trying to hide the baby?

I hope, you've given up smoking, completely, or must you burn your lungs to believe in yourself? Study the cigarette smoke, see yourself evaporate ahead of time. I've watched the whirlpool in the rich red wine, and learned that breath is everything. Our words are its shape. Tell me your secrets now. I am the one who needs to know.

Love,
André

It's too late. I have been discovered. Many of my colleagues are fathers, and recognize the distress of pregnancy. One asked out of nowhere, in what month I am. Now my *Chef* knows. The regulations demand my removal, but his reputation protects me. Unaccountably my *Chef* liked you. He does not know that you disappeared the Russians. Perhaps, he wants you to take him too. You left your influence here, most of all on Frowin.

He has grown strange. You are his *Führer* now. More and more my cousin, like you, believes in the idea of Germany as the failure of its own complexity. 'Just as there are special cancers caused by low-frequency radiation that create the brain itself as a cancer, so too Germany has grown into consciousness, a cancerous revelation not to itself but to the rest of the world.' Frowin tells this to everyone who will listen, as you do. They think him crazy, as they did you.

Odo has joined the autonomous too, but as a provocateur, to give them a bad name. Both he and Frowin are now known Autonome, an alias for anarchists. This is not a contradiction. They practice the circle A brand of wall art. Both wear black leather jackets, boots and pants, checkered chadahs, and black ski masks with red eye slits. Yet, Frowin still believes with you in a more colorful society: he has dyed his hair green. My mother forbids me to talk to him. He is the black sheep in my family, but so am I, for going to America and wanting to believe that people are equal. But there are only black sheep in my family, yet we each believe, *Shander-bander, a kapore far eynander,* to use the criminal lingo of long ago: 'One is as bad as the other'. What do you think now?

And what is your plan for us? Do you have one?

Love, Sara

Dear Sara,

My plan? To haul you home, to the U.S., to reroot you, graft you in place, to the liberty tree, but I can't stay away.

I'm in London, en route, in the fire-warm den of my only living aunt. She's been nibbling frozen cherries and telling me family stories. I've learned that my mother was born in Edinburgh, out of wedlock, and that her mother ran away wealthy at 17 from Russia. In a green leather album are old family photographs, wonderful to see, made over a century ago in a blue-glass-roofed room, and inscribed on the back, "For think not these portraits by the sunlight made, though shades they are, will like the shadow fade."

That to me is poetry. I don't appreciate the modern variety. The electro-logic of the machine mind short-circuits itself so quickly. But what do I know? I'm just a 'likeness man', as photographers were first called. My focus is here.

I've found a treasure, equal to any. Indeed, materially, 4 of the daguerreotype portraits of my family are solid silver plated in gold, a practice common at the time. More importantly, I can add the British Isles to my heritage. Also, it seems, my grand-parents came from the same small town in Lithuania. Of different class, they didn't know each other there, however. Posh, posh, my aunt says.

I told her about us, about your lost past and my uncertain future. She said, "Every 50 years Germany blows its brains out. It should stay dead."

My aunt is a strong woman, in personality and prowess. She swam the Channel in her youth, but she doesn't look back. For her, England is the queen of cultures, and the rest of Europe as dry as dirt. She remembers Norway though as 1000 Yosemites. Definitely!

Still your André

Dear André,
Please, please, come out, come out, wherever you are.

You are being civil to the point of incivility! How long can you ignore my mother? You must talk to her about our plans. You do not have to ask her permission, but you need to present yourself to her. Do you really want me to spend the rest of my life squirming on Freud's filthy couch? She knows already, that you are a strange bird and a bad mouse catcher, and that accordingly I will not marry you, but you are overdue to face her. Formalities must be observed. I used to think everything conservative was awful, but not here and now. Well, what are you going to do about it? Your past is my past now, and I am your future, whether you like it or not.
Love,
Sara

Dear Sara,
If you return to the U.S. with me right away, I'll be happy to say good-bye to your mother. If not, you know more about what's going on than I do. When you tell her our plans, do tell me too.

Meanwhile, I'm still in London, but thinking more about Norway. I can show you the changing sights by cutting up my contact sheets into postcards. With clothespins, a sheet of glass, a scrap of red plastic, and an ordinary lightbulb, I can make story-boards or prints on demand, in most any bathroom.

Maybe your mother should meet my aunt. Would they find anything in common?
Love,
André

Dear André,

Surprise, surprise, yourself. My father liked your ideas on
converting. Vienna needs Jews. Converts are the best way to
bring them back. The few Jews residing in Vienna now are
Rumanian mostly, refugees stranded after World War Two on
the way to Israel, too poor to continue. They are uncultured,
artless, with by-the-book beliefs. There is a Jewish Museum but
it has only two employees, and one, the director, lives in Israel
and refuses to return to Vienna, even though the museum is
about to move into a large new building, donated by the city.

Our child could be the first of a new generation, yes?

Thanks for the postcards, but your efforts are pointless.
My destination is fixed. I am not voyaging anywhere. I hear
your objections to the baby being born here, but I disagree.
True, medical facilities are not equal to those in the U.S. Yes,
yes, the equipment is old, the sonograms have poor definition,
but do we need photographic quality? It is true, the herbalist
union exercises too much control and its members are wishful
as witch-doctors. But physicians puzzle with themselves too,
and experiment unnecessarily. We are not gods. Medicine is
only educated guesswork. If everything is normal there will be
no problems. Accordingly I have arranged my own room at the
hospital and the company of mid-wives around the clock. I do
not expect nor should I need the interfering hand of male doctors, but they will be available in an emergency. As far as I am
concerned, here is as good as anywhere. I feel comfortable. You
will be with me helping lovingly. You better be. The question of
the baby's citizenship can be settled when it is relevant. Till
then, the baby will be on my passport and traveling the world
with me. You can adopt her later. My mother of course wants
the baby to be born in Vienna.

I have been reading EMERGENCY, a new French novel

of social distress, in which there is no resolution, and little romance, only the old octopus of war-nerves as a way of life, groping all of us, endlessly, together.

I agree, that Germany is not swimming in its own tank yet. This country is a fat floating toy of Western intent. Yes, yes, its people have been happily fossilizing as spoiled children of the U.S. We have been allowed to play with ourselves. That is why my *Chef* always was anxious to know what you as an American think. But Germany has a chance to grow up all at once now, in the process of unification and, by renewing former alliances, be born once more. *Ja, ja,* this will lead to a restored belief in the explosive dominance of Central Europe over the rest of the world. You will have to fight us again. Most of this country, especially those with power, think they can escape the state of emergency and uncertainty the novel predicts for us all. As the heroine says, "I'm young, I'm supposed to be having fun. Instead I'm stressed out about everything, from my next breath to my favorite dessert." She sounds American, if you ask me, but then that is where Europe's current troubles begin.

I have gone traveling again, with my mother this time, as this might be my last trip with her. I do not know why, but I hoped to meet you, by accident, in the center of every city we visited, though I should have known better.

Then again, a half-million Russians still are hanging out at the resorts in the East and refusing to leave. They are bleeding Germany to dust. My mother says, that Moscow is complaining. It does not know what to do with the 100 trainloads of ammunition its troops brought with them. They can not ship anything back. Their seaports on the Baltic will not accept the weaponry. The troops say that they have nothing to go back to in any case. I have heard unofficially, that Germany has offered to pay eight billion Mark to build housing for the Russian troops, but in Russia. Poland in turn has kindly offered to accept every last weapon in East Germany. The Poles want a new wall, perhaps a box-car wall, of live ammunition, between themselves and anyone German. Of course, both Germanies think that the Pole is forever filthy, crude and criminal and must therefore serve his refined betters. This country insists on going backward, yet always it burns its bridges. Unlike England and France, it has no friends in the world, *nein*, even among its former colonies.

At the same time, a festering state of sedition gives an insidious aspect to serious enterprise. You know this is true. My father believes it too, that the West still is provoking the East to rebellion, while stealing it blind. Orchestrated, chaos, even revolution, are likely. Is that why you are here? Why can I not know where you are? I must know. Have you been searching for cameras or conspirators? Please, now is not the time to disappear.

My mother and I avoid talking about you, and men in general, my father included. She is learning the real world as a result, with a cynicism I thought her incapable of. Nonetheless, I will not expose my mother to the icy insults of your aunt.

Please do not be mad, that I'm taking my vacation with my mother. It is my duty.

My father is becoming concerned with his own mortality. He says he has much to accomplish first, but that ultimately he wants his ashes pressurized into diamonds and left on the black sand beaches of Namibia.

Where are you seeding?

Love,
Sara

Dear Sara,

I spent May Day in East Berlin, looking for you also. It was
the 100th anniversary celebration and the first year in recent
memory that attendance and marching weren't compulsory.
Nevertheless I expected a political showdown, tear gas, a free-
for-all. Nothing happened. Few Easterners came, yet it was
wall-to-wall people anyway. Most strolled in from the West,
to enjoy the unthreatening air, unfamiliar tastes, the luxury
of new leisures. The Platz was like a carnival fairway. The
Concessionaires got rich on the kiwi-coconut drinks at the
Brandenburg Gate. Imbiss stands competed at over-pricing.
Free sample cigarettes were everywhere though, and the Red
Cross offered hungry Easterners Bratwurst, bursting with fat.
Ein-Mark each. Nearby, beer-garden bands sang about the
fatherland while soldiers goosestepped at the tomb of the
unknown boot. And in a far corner, with less than 100 people
listening, a Communist band from Chile rallied the few
remaining faithful, around several under-dressed teenagers
parading as the future. Hopefully my images of the day will
enlarge your postcard collection and keep it unique.

Love,
André

Dear André,

Is she serious, the woman you photographed — with her behind sticking out of her shorts and a beauty contest banner hiding her lack of tits, but proclaiming her to be the first new Communist of the year? Your postcard is appalling. You don't care who you film.

In any event, I am tired of mailing three letters for you to get one. We must stop this travel dance. It is a waste of postage and paper. You can only be in one capitol at a time. Which is next?

love, Sara

Dear Sara,

I'm parading in Potsdam this week with the Russian Army. Their over-wide hats make them irresistibly self-conscious. In the morning, camera in hand, I'll visit the local castle to watch the bats leave as the tourists arrive, try out the recycled toilet paper and inspect the destiny lilies. Afterward I might find out the real difference between the purple and green diesel pumps in the gas stations. When I ask, the attendants answer, the gas is the same color as the pump, and the same under the color, but one you pay for in DM and the other in *Ost-Mark.* Not that it matters, the car runs on anything. The Russians made offers on it. I should've accepted, but I didn't want to be paid in uniforms. Now the radiator leaks. More repairs are needed. Are you mad that I took the car out of storage without first asking? I figured, that your mother's new Audi is your preference anyway. Did she give it to herself as a retirement present? She's breaking it in for you and the baby, I'm sure.

Love, André

Dear Sara,

On Tuesday I called till 3 in the morning, to tell you to expect me. No one answered. Are you all right, have you found a new father for the baby — what circles are you going in now? Try answering me. There's no point in postponing trouble. This is the second time I've called late and you weren't there. Are you with friends? Will they stay up all night with the baby too? Blowing smoke in your face, to put it to sleep?

What's going on? Am I still the baby's father? I'm waiting for any answer.

love,
André

Dear Sara,

I've been driving all night, on my way to you, straining to see through the yellow bug juice on the windshield. No road lights or edge markers in this eastern land. Curves are unfamiliar. Coal dust veils the windshield, dims the headlights, and chokes the engine too. I intuit the route much of the time.

Now I hear, forebodingly, that another sun-grazing comet disappeared this week. Were you and Nili at it?

love,
André

"Listen — "

"No, André, you listen. I have had enough. Your worrying about me has me worried about you. I do not need nut-calls in the middle of the night."

"Then tell me what's going on?"

"Nothing. I do what I have to."

"Really. Well I've been thinking. It's ridiculous. Why should I have to adopt my own child? "

"Because you are in my mousetrap now."

"In the U.S., if you're born there, you're a citizen, simple as that. Let's just go!"

"Your country can not tell us who is a citizen here. It is not allowed. Besides, as my mother says, the U.S. has no culture."

"Whose child is this anyway? How do you know?"

"Are you trying to get me angry?"

"I called at midnight last night. You weren't home."

"You make me miserable. I make myself happy. My friends console me. My mother does not."

"Am I anywhere in your picture?"

"I brag about you to the women and complain about you to the men. I get lots of sympathy."

"I'll be there in a few hours."

"No. Not yet. Yes, yes, Nili arrived this morning, and I want to talk to her without you."

"Meaning?"

"I'm going to find out the truth. And I do not want you around till I do."

"What truth?"

"Why you want me to feel guilty?"

"That's easy. When you feel guilty, I wonder if you have reason to."

"So, you're only jealous! I wish I were stronger, so you

could not manipulate me. You destroyed my defenses, I do not relate to children. Why should I have one?"

"I didn't get past your defenses, you did. You hardly had any anyway. You were a raw nerve. Past rejections hurt you that deeply. You're like your mother now, rejecting the world in turn —"

"Well, there is no reason for me not to have a baby, as long as it is a girl."

"Who said it's going to be a girl? Every woman I know who resembles her father, even superficially, has had boys."

"When I look in the mirror I see my mother."

"Is that why I'm the enemy?"

"No, it is because you got me pregnant."

"Did I? I wonder. Definitely. Sometimes I suspect more than one man, perhaps the *Vaterland* itself."

"You bastard!"

"Even if you haven't hopped into bed with anyone else, the idea of the fatherland certainly has scummed up your mind."

"Pig! My mother would kill you."

"Tell her, she doesn't have to, we'll never get married, no matter what. She'll be happy."

"Nothing makes her happy. My father wants us to be united though. He does like you, no matter. He wants you to write to him too. He has time for you. But I do not want you to, unless I see the letters first. Do you understand?"

"No. You're driving me nuts. Is this a hormonal highway that we're on?"

"Yours or mine, Mr. André?"

Dear André,

I am ignoring our last conversation, for the baby's sake. But why is it that we talk more when we are not together, than when you are here? I admit, I may be somewhat responsible too, but responsibility is not my forté. Blame is, and you must accept that.

Nili says, hello. Odo says, thanks for Nili. You brought her. He may regret himself tomorrow, but today he is in love. She is snubbing him. He is beside himself. They met in argument. Nili can be testy. She has geometry problems at NASA. She worked on turning a sphere inside out without creasing it, and on changing a circle into a square, only to learn, that a Hungarian mathematician beat her to both. Odo is electronically engaged, to this planet. He is now constructing nerve docks, for smart bricks, in the connecting skin. He complained, that Nili was indulging herself with simple isolated problems, instead of participating in the greatest research of our time, so well funded in the U.S., the study of genes, and the creation of new species, like the Harvard mouse. He was jealous and angry at the possibilities denied him. 'Why should the U.S. own all the patents?' he wanted to know. 'The genetic alphabet only has four letters,' Nili said, 'However you arrange them, they still spell f-u-c-k.' Odo has never met an uninhibited American before. She is an entirely new genus to him. She cleaned his laser printer in the lab, with an air gun, for her own use, and charged him, in aerosols. After collecting, she said, "Pardon my French but you just paid $85 for a blow job." Odo proposed to her on the spot. They talk to each other through me when they

do talk. I am their translator. Odo wants to do gene research at
Los Alamos. He saw a job ad, for U.S. citizens only. I admit
Odo has his problems. His mother starved him as a fetus, to
keep her figure, then overfed him as a baby. She raised a cranky
bully-to-be as a result. He suffers indigestion always. But if you
bundled him with the Russians, or if Nili divorced and married
him, he would qualify for the secret side of Los Alamos, yes?
Unfortunately she regards Odo as a spin-forbidden transition.
The barrier energy of belief walls them in different states of
being. She is interested in the Russians though, in the four that
are left, bodily interested, yes, sexually as well as in their work,
on a blue laser using transparent metallic hydrogen as buffers
between crystalline platinum mirrors. No, she does not ask
me to translate when she is in bed with them. I think, she is
working on a new geometry, to create a saddle shaped interface
in a five bubble cluster, though that contortion has been
achieved also, mathematically. Odo wants the Russians
deported. He is informing on them, to their government.
How male!

You should be glad that you are somewhere else.

Outside my window, a hopping bird is pecking bugs out
of the air. Yes, Nili is here.

Love,
Sara

Dear Sara,

Nasty, nasty, aren't we? I met Nili as she passed thru Prague, where I've been in retreat, and heard her version of things. She called your cousin Odo, His Odiousness, but also said, she envied you, your peaceful pregnancy. She admits to falling in love with Svedlini, the lanky Russian from Leningrad, and inviting him to the U.S. He's traveling with her now. Strangely enough, he's free to. "I want to say," he said, "everything before now was Stalinist. We are instructed, but don't now have to listen. The first time to leave is the hardest. Russian society is very complex, very layered. In Soviet society nothing is simple. I have a wife and child of 7 waiting. It's been very pretty talking to you. Do you think I must go home?"

It's time I was returning also. It's always time, but I seem never to get there. Nonetheless, traveling I can only find the familiar now. In West Berlin a child's party in a McDonald's ended with a parade of ad waving. The western flood washes well. East is easier, but there are no horizons, nothing beyond the here and now anymore. Day after day, the infinity point is so quickly arrived at. Drought, diminishing returns have set in, I've stopped photographing. The common changes are crust, but salt grows nothing. Social blisters will yet erupt, and drain, for sure. Criticism will boil too, but eventually the people will accept, that with kiwis comes cocaine, with democracy come skinheads. Right, I've been talking to your father. Can I come back now?

Definitely, in both Germanies, there's no escape. Even the quad sound of nature is overwhelmed. People walk around in a shock of attention, with *Achtungs* posted everywhere, in the crowded campgrounds.

Curiously, your father found me, in Prague. He must have considerable influence. Am I being watched? He came in a

well-equipped camper, that reminded me of a traveling court-
room, with its barred windows and dark-wood paneling. I told
him, Nürnberg was advertising for a Professor of Crime and
Punishment, he should apply. On his desk was the South
African Digest, and on its cover was a mocking cartoon of a
humanized globe with its arms and legs crossed, covering the
pubic South African region. Namibia was once part of South
Africa too, it seems. I asked your father his purpose. He said, he
was buying grave-sites, in the same way Germany is buying
garbage dumps in other poor countries, now that East
Germany is *verboten*. I don't know who's jiving who anymore.
He took me to a lodge and ordered eagle for dinner and dessert
wine. "I live to be drunk every day of my life," he said soberly,
and then very seriously asked to be called by his "first name,
Norbert, pronounced without the T, as in French." Then he
said, a mistake had been made and he wanted to correct it,
but he must've changed his mind, because he passed out with
his sixth drink. I dumped him into his trailer. In the morning
he was fresh as a tulip. I found him in front of his TV. "I want
to see if East Germany has a government yet," he said. As you
must know, conservatives endorsing unification won everywhere. But the scales are skewed. In many cities all the super-
markets are being sold to a single chain, so again no competition is possible. Consequently, the population flow is still west,
with fewer and fewer going east, to buy or visit. The Easterners
are Europe's new vagabonds. Should I join them or remain in
limbo with your father?

It's easier talking with him now. He loves to talk, and even
to sing. He said that his grandfather conducted a military band,
and choked to death on a piccolo reed. Your father hums tunes
I've never heard. Are they original, or your family's link to an
ancient marshy alpine past? He won't tell me.

love, André

"No, no. You will come back, but first you must make peace with my father. He is a man of influence, and important to me also, even when I despise him. I know that I'm contradicting myself. I do not want you to see him, but you will. Life is short and secrets are long. You must learn ours."

"Whether I want to or not? Hell, I feel like a pendulum. I swing toward you and away, day after day, but never touch or rest at your side anymore."

"Now isn't the time. Soon perhaps I will need my belly kissed again. You must wait for me to want you."

"When will that be? Hell — when your safety shield at work explodes? You're in constant danger. Hydrochloric acid seeps even from a stoppered bottle. I know what you're doing in the lab."

"It is my last chance, please. Who told you?"

"Nili, and the Russians."

"The traitors."

"Aren't we all supposed to be on the same side these days?"

"In what fantasy are you living?"

"Yours."

"Then you know what you have to do."

"No."

"Find out. I will not wait forever, or even two weeks. My father is more dangerous than my chemistry, and you must neutralize him. Do you understand?"

Dear Sara,

I left, then doubled back on myself, to Prague, to test your
father. He's slick. I thought I was. I used his name to register
my camp-site, in a different more-remote sparsely-wooded
park. He showed up late at night and told the guard that I'd
been paid only to come ahead to reserve his space. I was evicted
and slept in the back seat of the Mercedes. You're right, your
father's influence is frightening. His access suggests iniquity.

This morning your father apologized, then sat me down
with his newest stamps. In the U.S., stamps celebrate, com-
memorate and sell. Here they pronounce government policy.
Yes sir, amend history and constitutions by mail. The largest
Germ stamp this year proclaims the "40 year charter of those
Germans expelled from their homeland:" i.e., Poland and
Czechoslovakia. The Vienna press published the competing
designs for the stamp, showing most of Poland as part of
Germany. The Czechs now apologize for deporting their
Germans after the war, even the ones Hitler sent in as settlers.
The country is hungry, they eat boot. I say what I want here.
The Czechs agree, with smiles and shrugs. A hundred million
Mark of German charity buys lots of crow.

Indeed your father admits to a condescending fondness for
the Czechs. Their embassy in East Germany helped plot the
independence. By housing dissidents, for bloated fees from
the Bundesrepublik, the Czechs tangled the Communist web.
Definitely, or so he says.

Again I asked him his purpose. He answered, to keep me
out of trouble. I told him, I'd nothing to lose. *Fa !* your father
said, spitting out a pit. We were in a proper cafe, with two ash-
trays, one for cherry pits and the other for cigarette stubs. Your
father filled both. We talked a long time but to no conclusion.
Will I ever know or find what I'm seeking? Will he?

André, your lover still

My father is alert to you. Stop pretending to innocence. He is testing you too, preparing you as he must. You should not be so routinely antagonistic toward him, or Odo either. My cousin saved my life, yes, yes, and the baby's! He did.

Every Tuesday I attend a night belly-dancing class for pregnant women. I am staying in shape for you, I am. Last evening I walked through the town square as usual, window shopping and thinking good thoughts about us, when I came upon a demonstration against a Greater Germany. According to the press of today, 8,000 police lined the march route of 2,500 protesters. At first there was no action, only a show of uniforms on both sides, each wearing their black leather jackets, pants and boots. The anarchists stood closely in rows of ten across, clinging to heavy manila guide ropes, that bound the first one hundred rows, into a human battering ram, whose aim was to break the police lines, by mass momentum. More people came, slowly pushing the front forward. They chanted in accented English, 'Hold on! Hold on! Hold on!' and 'Smash, smash, smash the State!' I watched, as you might perhaps, fascinated, spell-bound really, forgetting that I was pregnant. The two forces styled themselves so similarly. Only the head-gear was different. The police wore hard helmets with lifted visors. The anarchists stared through knitted ski masks, but I could tell by the bulge of their hips, that the front-line was entirely women. They surged forward, swaying. Waiting thirty meters ahead was a very different group of police, with clubs but no shields, wearing loose olive-green wind-breakers over flack vests stuffed with grenades. Suddenly I realized the dan-ger: I stood in the way! These police sneered and glared right through me. Contemptuous, angry, they fixed on targets and tensed to attack. The marchers inched forward. The police waited, in a state of vicious alert. Trapped between them I fainted, and fell. My head hit the bricks, which bruised but woke me. Odo kneeled to me. He had broken through somehow. On his shirt was a red cross, the top arm a raised fist with a bandaged thumb. His immunity saved me. The special police squad charged into the column of marchers, splitting the center, crippling everyone in reach, and killing a woman in the fifth row. The panic of the anarchists fragmented the surrounding police line. The marchers raced off, through side streets, smashing the mannequined windows of fashionable stores. Waiting though were right wing fraternities, well dressed, with long knives. Other police, ready for anything, dropped from the rooftops, to save the anarchists. The fraternities fled. All the while Odo shielded me. He was clubbed, trampled on, and cut. I have never seen him so proud of himself. I went home with a minor headache, that is all. He stayed. Today's newspaper said, the dead woman was shot by an unidentified sniper. No, it was not Odo, and perhaps not the police after all. In fact they claimed only to be protecting the anarchists in their unpopularity, and to have been there for just that reason. *Ja, ja.* Do you remember the kidnappings at the 1980 Olympics in Munich? The anti-terrorist squad killed the hostages as well as the terrorists. Sharp fellows: bullets can not be contradicted. Besides the hostages were Jews.

Incidentally, Odo claims to be cured of Nili. I hope you too have seen the light. I tell you again, I do not mind what you do, but do not dare have other children.

Being pregnant, I am not as judgmental anymore, I admit. I do not have the energy. I have lost interest in events also.

If I had read the paper, I would have known not to pass
through town yesterday. As the world inside me grows fuller
and I rounder, I dream more about us. In three weeks, when I
reach my seventh month, I will need you to lean on, to balance
my increasing awkwardness. I do not want to roll down the
marble stairs at the lab. There is always the elevator of course,
but it is so small. No one else can ride with me now. My *Chef*
complained, the department is too fecund, producing more
babies than science. Many of the men visit their wives daily in
the maternity hospital.

While in Prague, you should visit the Street of the
Alchemists. It is famous. When the Emperor Rudolf died, his
treasury held four tons of gold and three of silver. This was
probably the last of the Hapsburg spoils of Mexico and Peru,
but its existence is an enduring mystery. I came to chemistry
through history and alchemy. They are related, do you know?
I used to believe, as the books taught, that chemical essences
released powerful social forces, like the French Revolution.
But it was a golden colored distillate called the Sperm of the
Alchemists that fascinated me most. Then I grew up. But there
is no denying the power of sperm. Look what it's done to me.
Worse, Odo told me today that he is more man than I am
woman, so he is entitled to greater pride. I was dismayed. He
said that, when a woman is pregnant, her mind seeps away and
only after her baby is born does she regain some brain but, like
a reptile's tail, it never grows back entirely. I will slap his face,
maybe, tomorrow.

Pictures of the confrontation that nearly crippled me are in
every newspaper. There will be more opportunities for your
camera, when you get here.

love,
Sara

"You're all right, you're sure? Did you see a doctor?"

"Yes. 'Put ice on the outside, aspirins on the inside, and go to sleep,' he said."

"I should be there."

"I am managing, I still work. I am capable."

"Really? What's new in the molecule market?

"I would not know. Business makes new molecules, science dissects them."

"Are your anarchists under study also? How can they march in line, in uniform, and still call themselves —"

"You do not understand! These are German anarchists!"

"'I see,' said the beer-blind."

"Are you examining your life also?"

"No, just my bank account. Camping's expensive here."

"Saves on the culture shock, though, yes? But why are you camping? This is Europe, not California!"

"Keeps me closer to the caves. Your father suggested, I find places to stay through the waitresses in the cafes."

"He did? Is he cheating on his new wife already? What do you do for company?"

"Call you, write to you, touch people with my eyes, photographing."

"You missed a fine picture of Odo, wounded, printed in *Stern*. The streets are portrayed as more dangerous daily."

"Probably. But nothing's as frightening to me as the lab you live in. I know you're still working with explosive potentials. I don't say anything because you won't listen. So I keep traveling, coming and going, as you ask. Or I'd sit there fretting, and charge into the lab, to pull you out in front of your colleagues, to your endless embarrassment. I have to believe, you know what you're doing, and trust you, and assume you trust yourself, even if I'm wrong."

"Good. Good. You must encourage me, always. Please, remember to. Come back for awhile. The baby is still inside. I'm lonely."

"Can I use the lasers in your lab?"

"To rob a vault?"

"To test a new pair of lenses."

"You will go blind."

"Then I better take a good look at you first and maybe make some new pictures."

"Yes, yes, I will let you. It will be a chance for you to see me differently. I have been thinking. It is as if I am from the West and you from the East. Can your photographs unify us too?"

"Curious. I think of myself as the Westerner and you as the East Reichian."

"*Nein.* We are suburbs of Berlin, like everyone else. We are losing any other choice.

"Who's we, white woman?"

"Stop mocking. Come home. I need you."

"Okay. But I won't see the Street of the Alchemists. That's okay by me, I guess. The soul of gold is the sun. That's the only alchemy I believe in."

"One day you will believe in me."

Spending three weeks with you reassured me, only because nothing's changed. Your belly grows so slowly. And your father is following me again. Definitely. Did you ask him to? We're in Berlin. He keeps asking what I'm doing. I'm not sure myself, but I showed him contact sheets from my wanderings. He wanted prints immediately. I told him he'd have to wait. He guided me to a private darkroom, then to the Goethe Institute. Reluctantly I went. Much to my surprise, the plain-dressed director enthused about my imagery at first, but in the end grew as grim as the photographs and said sternly, "Our Chancellor would not be happy with your views of us. Where are our Yuppies in their BMWs? That's what Americans want to see!" I saw more heroin addicts shooting up on the street in Frankfurt, and more homeless in the Hanover railroad station than Yuppies. "But I didn't photograph any of them, as I was focused on every-day normalcy," I said, lying. "I even ignored the BMW's on their backs in single-car accidents, on your Autobahn," I went on. Sourly the director offered help, in the form of support for a show in the U.S.

Your father was delighted. He produced the glass plates that you'd warned me about, as if he and I had something more in common now, than just you. "This will be our little secret. You may keep them for me," he said, grinning.

You've seen them, of course, haven't you? Transparent images in black & white, made with a 5x7 view camera, maybe during The Great War. They still shock — displaying victims, close-up, torn and bloodied, mangled and emaciated, alive! I don't know what to think. Who made them, why were they saved, does your father believe the pictures valuable? Is this your dowry? You knew, you definitely did. Why didn't you warn me fully or hide them forever? I told your father that

because the images are fading toward orange, brown and
purple they look like strange stained-glass windows, and
I wondered aloud about worship and marriage. He laughed
without answering, and went on drinking a wine that he
didn't share, a kirsch, that requires 3,000 cherries a bottle.

Do you know about the Gestapo-forced-march through
Germany in the closing days of World War Two? The starving
bodies of captured British pilots literally digested their own
hearts. My aunt's husband, my uncle, was among them. Only
the malicious could enjoy such similar sights. The details of
an ever-lasting death are devilish, even to doctors. Your father
isn't old enough for World War One. Does he wish he was?
"Is Vienna even sicker than Freud said?" I asked. Your father
is proud. He smiled ever more widely, with his nose in the air,
but refused to answer. I began to wonder, why most everyone
in your country enjoys wearing the same straight jacket.

And then suddenly, in a moment of doubt, it struck me
that the glass plates could be captured photographs instead.
The format, the measurements, are British or American. But
your father wouldn't confirm or deny my suspicions. Are the
families in the photographs German after all? I know that east
of Berlin, now, small mass graves are being opened, to uncover
more recent Russian atrocities. "Who are these people? Are
these my ancestors, or yours?" I asked your father. He still
wouldn't answer. He continued drinking his kirsch. In the
silence, I thought awhile, trying to second-guess him. "Are
the glass plates evidence toward reparations?" I asked.

"No, these are not Jews or Gypsies," he finally said in
disgust. "Who's to know?" I asked. "Even so, $450 is the most
we could expect for each," he said flatly.

"Can we claim a block of East Berlin anyhow?" I answered.

"Impossible. It is not allowed. The dignity of a country is
in its borders. Reparation is a personal matter."

"Exactly," I said, "The surviving few deserve the sections of East Berlin that were theirs."

"We would have little Israels everywhere," he said, horrified.

"Certainly," I said, "Why not? The ghetto wasn't Hitler's invention. Officially designated negative space, it deserves special privilege, even renewable independence, within the larger community. Can I be mayor?" I asked.

My enthusiasm for the scheme enraged him.

"You toy with me!" he said, "You have no respect!"

"We can call ourselves the Tribe of Berlin, claim the land as Fort Israel, and sell it to the Russians," I went on.

"So then, Mr. Jew!" he answered, angrily, "Prove who you are! Where are your papers?"

"Why should I need any?" I asked and laughed at his leering demand. For a Germanic Catholic culture to decide who is a Jew and issue identity papers accordingly struck me as gibberish or mummery at best. Yet his question reminded me of my ex-wife, the woman you first saw on my wall. She now has a certificate saying that she's sane. It was issued by the insane asylum. No one else I know has such papers. Still in the U.S. you are what you say you are, till proven otherwise. You're allowed to reinvent yourself, innocently.

If your father didn't like his kirsch so much, I think he'd have thrown the half-full bottle at me.

So, I mailed the glass plates to the Holocaust Museum in Washington D.C., as a present, in your father's name.

I hear Germany is considering a new program, as its remembrance. Adopt a Dead Jew! I.e., one who died in the camps. Lists are being compiled by unemployed ghouls, i.e., historians. Yeah!

love, André

"Your letter left me in shock for two days. But you did right.
André, I am sorry. I know next to nothing about the glass plate
pictures. I do not want to know either. I do not understand
how my father is oriented sometimes. I wonder then if he
is my father, but always my mother insists that he is. She used
to enjoy his outrage. She just could not keep up with his
mistresses. Please do not be like him. He is not a bad man
though, as far as I am aware. You handled him well, thank
goodness, but do let him spill the table on you too. We will
need him. Really he is only a simple believer, like me, but he
does not act. Were you so surprised?"

"By the glass plates? No, I expected them, I guess."

"You should have sold them to the Goethe institute then.
They may have guiltily paid."

"And dip my hands in the blood also? I couldn't. The angle
of vision was wrong. The cameraman modeled the wounds
delicately, as if he were in love with them."

"They were strangely appealing, weren't they?"

"The Middle Ages lives on."

"The Middle Ages ended in 1492."

"No, my dear, church feudalism continued alot longer.
Germany's still rebuilding the dark spires of its past, definitely,
and not-so-secretly loving its future crypts."

"André! You must stop. Why is the world so against
Germany? Only 5 percent of its people vote to the right of
the right-wing."

"Three percent can control a land of silent sympathizers.
That's the German theory. Your own petrified people in their

mold-green coats still peer down the human ladder, and give the million-and-a-half kids they helped murder a claim —"

"Stop it! That is propaganda! You will not change my beliefs. What about your father and the English camera he so admired, that the lord made out of his wife?"

"You have one arrow, faithful defender — "

"I feel middle-aged already, if you must know. I will be another PhD housewife soon, thanks to you."

"Can we go back to the U.S. then? I've looked enough. I'm finding no nests or safe harbors, only visions of doom here."

"Yes, yes, I am disappointed with here too, but I heard of a couple, who moved around the world to be safe, before the last European war, to a Pacific Island called Guadalcanal."

"Bad luck. But the island is green again, and the blood gone."

"Yes, except I am in mother mode at the moment. It is hard to be anywhere at all, and be wide awake, but I am comfortable here. I do not want to make changes yet."

"And I thought, you and I were going to be an adventure in chemistry together."

"We are, do not ever doubt it. The giant molecule growing inside me is you."

"Sounds exciting."

"Come home then. My father says, that a man can not be without a woman for more than two weeks, so I should not keep you away. Is he right? Must I marry you? I might if you would kiss my belly button every night."

The Myth of Mother's Milk

Welcome to the System: World Windows-tm
PENT/SUB/BAS/ARL/SL
user name? *******   access password? *******
Connecting to server in Apple Talk zone "Building 21"
Connecting to Mail-Pass: You have 3 unread messages
NILI@PLWARS.BITNET   July 15,16,17 9:00 AM
WW&: Pread   >Invalid command: Type H for help<
AO/EZ/Cursor Cntrl   Scan messages for capture

===

=+++=

WW&: Send
To: NILI@PLWARS.BITNET
Subject: Error-in-Progress
Cc: SYSTEM/DX-2/CPU
Bcc: DEFAULT/AO

Dear Nili,

Summer arrived in mid-August. The scene changed instantly.
On the street, green-haired beggars from East Germany crossed
the border to hassle the corduroy-baby-carriage crowd. Wasps
moved into counter cases at the bakeries. Mice are visiting us,
during the day now too, and eating the red pepper dikes I built
to keep them out. Mouse pee cakes the cayenne. All the little
domestic insects, of the heart and hearth, are thriving. Even
Sara bought diapers, feeding bras and a maternity blouse.
Believe it or not, intimations of domestic bliss resonate
through the house now and again, momentarily.

　　With the heat, thankfully, nudity is in vogue. Bare-feet
ungruntle the goose-steppers, but the quarry swimming hole,
with its contaminated water, raises rashes. Yet, at the lakeside
beaches, sun-happy, topless pregnant women play appealingly,

till black-tip dicks and ugly butterfly come along, to give a closeup face to the truth. Curiously though, just as Persians, even the most unsightly, have their eyes, so German women still assert their tits.

Yup, I'm photographing. With a show assured in the U.S. now, thanks to your agenting, I've made significant progress with the Goethe Institute. The propaganda agency was forced to sign on as a sponsor, to promote its presence. Protected by its always-above-us-all attitude, the Institute umbrellas Germany, in all things German, exposed abroad.

But I've managed on my own also. *Stern* may present my photographs, as a six page spread, "Through the eyes of an American". The idea of showing Germany to itself intrigues me. Besides which, I like what I've done.

It's good, I think. Curiously, there's an advantage to not understanding the language too well. Unable to read the newspapers yet, I miss the political grand-standing, the sponsored views, the business of business. Not watching television, I miss the head-ache inducing tone of events, the aspirin selling of the news. Without media focus, I avoid the timed release, and the selective eye of paid video-men. I get to see beyond the limits of the public lens, to what their videos don't show, each other at work narrowing the field of view. I can allow myself to look at the non-performance side of things also. I don't have to be a spectator facing a stage. I can watch the audience, the way it sees itself, privately.

Plots surface nevertheless, in the stiff similarity of gestures, the common rasp of expression and the guttural cast of voice. Regardless, daily life is infinitely varied and subtly undramatic, always. For the aggressive there are new sales opportunities and open touring now, but life has changed little. As Sara also says, freedom is a media experience first, and a shopping opportunity next. Today a West German woman can stuff her face equally well in East Germany, and claim a charitable contribution in the bargain.

My father's worn Leica has served me well. I wanted a quiet camera that also observed in the dark without special lighting, but still it was necessary to find my way by experiment. At first I let the camera surprise me, let it show me what it saw. It's true, I only discovered my method in the process, but thankfully the photographs reflect this blind seeing. They're slices of thought, slim black & white postcards to myself, like messages left by me on my own answering machine, from wherever I am, as a reminder, when I get home, of how I was lost or found.

Of course I participated while seeming not to. Photography is very like archery, you have to know when to let the arrow fly, when you have only a dozen and the armies of sight gather on you. There's a Zen to the camera, you learn to use it unthinkingly after a time, to zone your focus as well as your exposure and that way not touch or change anything, just go for the vision. I prefer the samurai approach, the stillness of the sword while the eye stalks, then the sudden single definitive stroke, after long practice the painterly slash. The impulse now feels natural, final, clean. Definitely.

And so should end my winter of darkness, compared to my time in the Marina light. But I'm still here, yes, hating this place. The coming baby keeps me, and Sara keeps me satisfied, even if she worries that my sperm may give her food poisoning.

I can't say that Germany's to my taste either. For sure, it needs a vomiting. I make no secret of my contempt. No one says boo yet, but walls are marked, Germany for Germans! Hail the Greater Germany! Foreigners Out! (in German of course). I've been painting five pointed stars over the messages, to remind everyone, this is a defeated country, and will remain so in all living memory. No one has stopped me. Of course, as a graffiti editor, I work only at night.

I have to admit, sometimes I think I'm going a bit crazy. I take a certain perverse pleasure in hating everyone here and antagonizing them, but it's a sport, which I can't lose. Sara says I must watch out, I will be stabbed and mortally wounded, but she has it reversed. My antagonists should be careful. I've had to restrain murderous impulses in myself more than once. It'd be so simple to give in to them, I'm still a ghost here. People ask me directions, offer supermarket credit cards, want my signature on petitions, till they hear me speak, then I disappear.

I'm beginning to think, killing Germans, blackening Germany, is a rite of passage, which every generation must repeat. Let the rage of injustice boil up and burn away the hate.

Of course I don't see our government making this a matter of policy, but then again you and I are the government, not the magpies and ravens in Washington.

If Sara and I convert, we'll have good excuses. Young Germans study Jews as trolls, as quaint and cute and unreal. Indeed Sarah, the name Hitler assigned to all Jews, is the most popular in Germany this year for newborns. Yes, Jews here are like Indians in the U.S., charming, wise and interesting, as long as they're near extinction locally, but alien, unnecessary, and destabilizing, when they form an enviable presence.

At the moment though, Jews have less to worry about than the more numerous Turks, or even the Japanese. Odo insists that both groups are hardly human. Even Sara doesn't relate. For the Russian poor, German high schoolers collect charity.

When next I'm in Austria, I'll paint the walls there too but with 6-sided stars. Austria is Germany's only real ally. The 2 countries define each other. Austria's the tail of the dog, and would wag the dog again. Mr and Mrs. Fossil, in their forest green camouflage, are the finger-pointing fleas to the last freehold. Certainly, Austria has elections, but we're talking eenie and meanie, minnie and moe, all toes on the same foot, since write-ins don't count, and you must vote, period, by party only, or an official calls on you to find out why, and fines you.

I'm sure Sara's ever-renewable need for autocratic control, her pinched embrace, is calculated to keep me here. To a degree she's succeeding. But the result is that I'm not only battling her, I'm combatting her whole culture, and wanting to fence and kill it. Germans, locked within their own borders, could only victimize each other.

Strangely Sara agrees with me, as if to keep me trapped. Her ambivalence about me seems calculated to stir the pot. She feeds on my frothing. Of course, in her lab, in parallel to her country's hemispheric search, she's now looking for the missing mass in the universe, hoping it'll be rare and valuable, but knowing that cold dark matter is the more likely find. (She explained, just as the sun holds the planets in place, so the planets hold the sun to its galaxy setting, but we can't see this because ordinary planets don't have light, heat or gravity sufficient to make themselves known to us.) But astronomical equations assume their existence. She admits however that, in the earthly moral polity, Germany itself and Austria too may well be the cold dark matter of Europe, wanting the sunny south as planets. She insists that I deny this, in the interest of peace, when we're arguing. Yet the definition forever stands, and keeps growing heavy metal feet.

No observatories of note exist in Germany, as there are no mountains, which explains the metaphysical reaching here, the abstract grasp from the very real swamp, and the elevated role of Switzerland & Austria.

Napoleon liberated Germany once, the Allies a second and a third time, but primitivism play well in this Neanderthal north. Large raw faces often give a sense of interbreeding.

I do think that the time will come again when the U.S. debarks here in force. I hope it's preparing. My presence doesn't count so far, really.

Odo and I argue too. His aggression grows by the day. "You lose every war, except with yourself," I told him. "Germany is a free country now!" he insisted. "You can never be free, you're German," I answered, and left him red faced and furious, stewing. Open assault is still beyond him for the moment. Of course he's a double e, Sara's slang for electrical engineer.

I hear Svedlini is planning to invite you to Moscow.

Summer meanwhile is fading already, too quickly. At the ice cream stand nothing's left now but *bum-bums* and *wuffs*, the first a raspberry disk, and the second a chocolate ice candle. Ah, for a creamsicle, or frozen orange juice, or just to be home again, in San Francisco. If you've explored, you know that the eastern edge of Russian Hill falls away steeply. The hill's like a wave forever poised to break, over Chinatown, but nothing that traumatic happens there, except in the quaking imagination.

The reality is, I'm afraid to admit it, I gave up a comfortable life on the crest of Russian Hill for a drifting dream cliff on a dark hungry sea, anxiously reaching for me. The ancient upwelling is cold. The currents rip at each other unceasingly. Whirlpools of change hide in small pockets.

Is this domestic bliss or what? At moments in fact Sara is serene. How long can it last?

Very soon, I hope, I'll be home. Meanwhile I'm still on the job. Spiderwebs make excellent cross-hairs.

André

>quit>
Disconnecting...
+++ a +++
NO CARRIER

Dear Nili,

Woman to Woman, I need your help.

I am glad André is with me, when he is, and glad that he is gone, when he goes. Our time alone is not recorded, and no one sees how nice he is to me. When he is not trying to prove himself, he is wonderful. I want everyone to know him at his best, but his worst is never far away. He keeps secrets too.

Yes, yes, André is up to tricks, as usual. I am not sure of what they are, but I know that you are assisting him. As a sister in womanhood I would appreciate your aid too. I have learned much, but I need to know many things more, from a U.S. perspective. André shares this with you.

Recently André is improving his behavior. I have decided to keep him. Tell me how I can hold him. I saw your effect on Odo. The subtleties of seduction escape me. I watch other women now. I pay attention, but no good ideas come to me.

In pregnancy, my body takes care of itself, but I am faced with changes daily. My breasts do not stop swelling. I do not know what to do with them, but I have choices now, new to me: to flaunt my enlargement, hide it, or position my globes outward, like a Roman goddess would. A wide X-banding between my breasts gives me a statuesque, distant, but availably naive look. This is inappropriate to the lab. A white blouse, plain black jacket, and a bun de-emphasize my chest, but make me matronly. This also is inappropriate at the lab. Which leaves cleavage. But I think that cleavage is bad as an attractor. Having cleavage is asking for someone to fall forward and unbind you. This too is inappropriate in the lab. What would you do?

I also need to know, as my father wants to join the far-right party publicly, whether there is a Jewish blacklist? My father is afraid, that his name may appear on it, and in turn cause me harm. You are Jewish, aren't you? I believe you are and your

husband too. He polishes expensive crystals all day long, but
his eye-glasses are always dirty. You smile too much for a Jew,
but your curly knotted magnetic hair is more you. I am simply
telling the truth. You understand, that I am serious. Please
excuse me if I have wrongly assumed to be true what may be
an insult, in your eyes.

André insists that a Jewish blacklist does not exist, but he is
no religion, so his answer is nothing. I need to put my father's
mind at ease. He is traveling with a West German economic
minister now, and helping to convince the East of the benefits
of transition. Nonetheless, my father and the minister console
each other often, about death mostly. I hope you do not
perceive this as insensitive, but the minister likes to say,
"No matter how many we killed, we still die too." You see,
my father's fear is only human.

My blemish is André. I do not know how to handle him.
I do not think that you do either, or he would be with you.
Problems are always many, and solutions few. You attempt to
deal with the world by being outgoing and optimistic. I am
withdrawn and negative. I am born to strive. Perhaps my
happiness is limited by my genes. Whatever I achieve is not
enough.

Today I wanted to put a *nix geht* sign between my legs. But
something always works for you. I want to know what it is. I
am not too proud to ask, while I'm pregnant, because I do not
care so much about anything right now. Nature is in control,
but I will regain the upper hand. I must.

My doctor says, nature has a louder voice than my mother
or André, and will not hear them, if I do not. The doctor said
too, sins can not be passed on. Thank goodness.

André though was born perverse. He is a snake biting his
own rattle, half the time. He has 20 skins under his own. What
should I do with him? What would you do? I have encouraged

him to keep photographing, but he sees harshly. I would see healing, if I knew how.

My father is to blame for not passing on to me the best that was. He is also learning to add André's perversity to his own.

You may think, that I'm bragging, now that my breasts are bigger than yours, but we are also sisters in science, so please help. You seek water in new configurations in space. I seek new metals, but I have fallen to earth. I dread the day my water bursts. In space, you could recycle it, for food and fuel. Here it will go down the drain.

In case of fire, destroy this letter first. I keep copies of everything. And say nothing to André. I will know if you have.

I am sorry that I called you a scientific dilettante, when you were here. You will find your place, I believe, when you stop moving from job to job and man to man. You should know better. Don't you?

Excuse my tone of frustration, please. I spent today cleaning, punishing the dirt. André will only bring home more. The people he collects in his photographs are incomprehensible to me. He likes sign forests and the like. You do know what I mean.

Yours,
Sara

Dear Sara,

Just a note from your main man, to tell you I'll be home late. Unexpected meetings and last minute arrangements. I'm on to something. Finally, a quick way to pay for our return together to the States — in one jump. I've been interviewing for this moment. The conclusion may come tonight.

Your father called, and called, and called again, first for you, then for me. He wanted you to know that whites will soon be begging on the streets in South Africa, if the U.S. succeeds in imposing its views there. "Life is a poozle," he said. I assume he meant puzzle.

Whatever his message, his introductions open doors, that seem to pay off. I'll fill you in later.

Nili called also. She was curt. She told me to tell you, there is no Jewish blacklist, but the U.S. keeps a data base with many uses, depending on the politics of the moment. She also said, you're fucked — that sour milk makes a bad mother — that your ego is your most swollen part. What's she mean? She wouldn't tell me. I didn't really want to get into the middle of a cat fight, but when I protested, to defend you, she hung up on me.

I spent most of the day in the darkroom at the lab, readying my exhibit. Can I include photos of you? No nudes. Nothing identifiable. Just your shadow, in our day to day life.

I'll be home soon, hopefully, my pockets stuffed with cash. Laugh, but don't be surprised at the sight.

love,
André

Dear André,

You must be wondering where I am, as I am the one who is gone now. I am writing this because I could not reach you by phone. There is bad news, I'm afraid. I'm sorry, that I left so suddenly. My mother is stricken. Doctors must stop her heart, to start it again to make her rhythm regular.

It is a stroke. Her left leg still twitches. Her left lung remains collapsed, but she improves 200% every day. Her self-timer is clicking again, but only toward the next explosion, as with my metals. I would wish you with me, but your presence might kill her. It's best that you are not here.

You will fend for yourself meantime. There is much food in the refrigerator. I arranged for you to use the laboratory darkroom indefinitely, as long as I see the pictures first. I do not know how long I will be here. My mother wants me to stay. After all, she has three bedrooms and a washing machine, and that is more than you can offer me. She says so, she knows. But I do not want to become my mother, and the baby needs a father, alas. I expect I will be home in two weeks, well before our child is born.

Nili is a cast off. A bad mold made her. She sent me a package of American bottle nipples because, she says, they breathe better and give babies less gas.

I am fine, though the bra marks on my shoulders get deeper every day. I priced baby carriages. They cost as much as a used car in the U.S.

I will miss the first day of German unity and the parties. Celebrate for me, please. See what you can see, and show me.

I know what I might want for a wedding present. Yes. In

San Francisco you served me grapes on beautiful hand-painted plates that said 'Made in Silesia' underneath. Were they inherited from your parents? Can I have them for my father, to replace the photographic glass plates which you took from him? I want him out of our lives. The oldest surviving dinnerware in my family is from 1943, heavy clay wartime issue, that my grandmother bought in Berlin. Everything else was destroyed by your bombs. You will grant my wish, yes? Tell me, was your father in the U.S. Army or the Russian? Did he bomb my family's dishes? My mother is convinced of this.

She also thinks that she must die for the baby to live, or vice versa. I could shoot her and Freud for putting such ideas in her head.

You may use my picture if it flatters me, if I don't look like myself, or if you have no other choice, and since I give you none, I expect to see myself in your show.

My mother is shouting at me now. She wants to know if she is my fault. She means, did she make me run away to you. Of course, she did. What should I say? Don't tell me.

My love to you,
Sara

The plates are yours. The earthquake spared them for you. In fact they were always yours. Somehow I knew you'd ask. Yes, they belonged to my father's mother. Yes, with his special skills, my father served the U.S., in intelligence, but the Soviets honored him also, for his aerial reconnaissance help.

As you wanted, I crossed the border Tuesday, to be there for the last day of the DDR. It was already dead. The stores posted signs, Please Buy Here! No one did. Women fled to the west for supplies. I drove northeast to the Harz Mountains. They're hills. They're bigger on a package of birdseed. Near the lakes, at the workers' resorts, were pictograms on roadside signs, insisting, No Tanks! I wanted the sign. I took it. Other Westerners were stripping the pear trees. At dusk I stumbled into a carnival in Quedlinburg and photographed the stand-up drunks, teenagers all. I guess the DDR difference is now, the police are on good behavior instead of the citizens.

Unity Day was Wednesday. Except for the full moon, nothing much happened here. Only the wandering Bolivians were out, the skin on their drums beat hairless, playing new age sounds, and dancing with each other in syncopated step. Many Germans stopped to clap, and tap their feet, as if to a waltz.

Now & again I watch TV, without the sound, to pass the time. The national highlight today was a "Cool as Fuck" rock concert, the sign waving above the crowd, in both English and German. Unification also seems to mean, that you can broadcast Hitler's favorite newsreels openly, without guilt, or anyone telling you not to. They're re-shown every day.

I'm sorry about your mother. I suppose some gesture is in order. Should I send Casablanca lilies?

I love you. André

"Sara, did I wake you? Are you all right?"

"Alles Gute, alles klar."

"Who are you talking to?"

"Oh. Oh, André, I was dreaming. I was talking to the André who speaks German."

"You sure you're all right?"

"No, I ate bad pancakes. Jelly donuts to you. My mother filled them by mistake..."

" — with infanticide cream?"

"No, buttermilk pudding that was spoiled. I am okay, but I will be delayed. The doctor just left, I think. Mama is nearly normal again. I am not. I wake up every morning, almost unable to move. My sleep feels drugged. I had my stomach pumped. It did not hurt the baby, the doctor said."

"You better come home, now!"

"I am too weak to travel. Besides, as my father says, what does not kill you makes you stronger!"

"Which father? Nietzsche?"

"I have only one father. I will eat out with him before I leave."

"And wear the Cross of the Iron Stomach, to the restaurant? Batshit isn't very filling."

"Stop it. You're not funny. It hurts me to laugh."

"I'm not laughing."

"My mother is taking care of me. She told me to say something nice to you."

"I'll be on the next train."

"No. Please, I will be all right. I have a few pickles, that is all. That is what we call pimples here."

"You need help."

"No. Times are good. We all have all, my mother says."

Dear Sara,

Did I miss your call? Were you out also? The warm night filled
the side lanes. Bicycle headlights, dimly disembodied, eased the
dark. They drifted unsteadily, like candles flickering. Winter is
almost here. The landscape's quickly fading. This morning I
picked the last blackberries near the road and wrapped them
in a dry oak leaf, the size of my hand, to carry them home.
A rugged woman, tense with courage, walking a small fox-like
dog, suddenly blocked my way, to ask a question. I answered, "I
only know English." She shook her head in despair. I couldn't
help but compare. People in the DDR practiced English eagerly,
however little they understood, whatever their politics.

At noon I lunched in a Chinese restaurant but strangely
the menu was Italian. I forgot that fungi here also means
mushroom. In the U.S. the difference is clear. One tastes like
seaweed, the other like a forest floor.

At home after an hour of skimming your laser journals,
I decided to build you a bookshelf to help make space for the
baby. But I found that every piece of wood in the lumberyard
was individually shrink-wrapped, and as expensive as sin in
Switzerland. My windfall of cash is delayed, but it's coming.

During supper I played with your computer. The matrix
printer sounds like a knife being sharpened. I guess I'll bus
back to the darkroom again, for company. I like waiting at the
butterfly painted bench. I've been dreaming of postcards to
send you, like storks on a checkerboard, and purple paisley
flowers in big brush strokes.

Hell, I'm here and you're gone. I don't feel right living in
your place without you, alone, still in limbo.

love, André

"André! Please! Stop playing with my lasers, when I'm not there! The lab may appear empty, but my spies are aware. You are under scrutiny, and for good reason, I tell you that. Who is the big woman, that you ate lunch with in the Chinese restaurant? My helper said, that she looked like a wanted poster, more than lost. Do you enjoy trouble?"

"I'm just being kind to your cousins in need."

"*Ja, Ja.* With my money?"

"No, with hers."

"*Ja, Ja.* Did she toy with you under the table too?"

"No, she has other tricks in mind."

"Huhu. But my mother will feed you anyway. She has made strudel skins for me to bring back."

"To turn me into a fat German or a dead American?"

"I want more of you. I like to play with your body. I like you when you have a high flu fever too. You become my hot lover again."

"Then tell the baby to hurry up out so I can get in. It wants to stay in there all by itself. It must be a boy."

"You can tell?"

"Inside you, I feel like I'm poking it in the head. Definitely, I'm sharing the space now."

"Good, good. You have too much free time. Why? You have darkroom work to do, for your show, to become rich. You will make money, the right way, no?"

"I make pictures, not money."

"But you sell them."

"Someone else will."

"You fell in love with my picture, but must live with the reality now and take it home to be diapered. You will not raise my baby in a suitcase."

"I see you're better too."

"Yes, and why are you in such a good mood?"

"I've been chosen, to do a good deed, because my rotten attitude's become famous."

"So that is what you intended! How will we bring up our child? My mother wants to know. What will you teach it?"

"The same as you."

"I would teach it tolerance in religion."

"Not me. I'd teach it to be intolerant, of all religions. They instill imperfection. I'd also teach the baby to disbelieve science, because it too promises the universe but only delivers broken atoms. I'd teach it to strike first, when threatened. I'd —"

"This is not what my mother needs to hear. Suppose I want the baby to be Catholic? They control more than Jews ever did here."

"To be Catholic you only have to take a bath. The Turks still will call you dirty-asses."

"You are a pig! Oh, I'm worried about us. You spoiled me into loving you, and now you are more cynical than me."

"No, I just have new opportunities. The U.S. is 200 countries, cooperating. Europe is twenty only, always clashing, in spite of the E.U. Austria too —"

"Stop it! I will not be condescended to in my own country."

"What's wrong? Are you crying? I'm sorry. Please Sara, be strong. You should take strength in us. We each want to be proud of who we are...I shouldn't be critical of you if I'm not holding your hand."

"It is okay. You need not worry. I know how important my
background is to me, I try to keep it in the background, yet still
you see it. I do not. But I will not fight with you anymore."

"You keep saying that."

"I want to mean it. It is hard. I am nothing, just another
pregnant post doc now, waiting for my life to end. I should fill
a balloon with acetylene and — "

"Sara! You can't be the only child forever."

"I realize, but I enjoy home. The roof comes down to the
ground in the rear. And there are many, many doors, to shut
yourself in or out. It is so private."

"And predictable, like the spindly woods outside?"

"Oh, our lives are so different. Are you sure you love me?
I should not ask, I am glad you do, that is enough. You far
exceed my demands. 'Photography is language,' you say so
often. *Nein.* It is dreams. Where are you now?"

"In the darkroom."

"What is it like?"

"Here? Dark. Too dark. Between the blue cold-light
enlarger and the amber-yellow safelight, I can barely see.
Even my memory of the image I'm making is cloudy to me.
Definitely. The warm thiosulfate, that I use for fix, stinks. My
sinuses are stuffed. In San Francisco the fog helps me see inside
myself, brings visions to me, but here —"

"Could I share your life there and observe what you see?"

"You're not trained to it. It's not photography that I do.
What's going on is something I can't teach, or really show
you. It happens like breathing, or birth, without thinking,
or direction. The camera's only a trigger."

"So, so, are you a love-assassin then? Did your camera kiss
me pregnant? The sleeping lens you sold me woke a world in

me that had died, but I'm taking my mother to the Museum of Twentieth Century Art tomorrow."

"There's modern art in Austria?"

"Yes, it is American...*Ja, Mama...Ja, Mama, ja, nein, danke.*"

"I'll call you back."

"No. She always stands over my shoulder. But we have talked a long time. How will you pay for this?"

"I won't. It's your phone bill. Besides, I dropped a hundred mark at the post office today. The price of exile."

"Szo, szo...My mother noticed the V-marks on my chest from my bra. She bought me new ones. She is most concerned with my breasts."

"How's she doing?"

"The doctor said, she is near normal again, she does not need me, but he did not tell me in front of her. Before I leave, I should take my mother for a mammography test."

"What'd the doctor say about you?"

"Nothing, but I already know, you are the strange bird and I am crazy too."

"Well then, come back soon and make yourself happy!"

"I will, to keep you away from my father. You must stop competing with him for me. You have already won. I am pregnant, remember? How often do you forget?"

"Yeow!"

Every day you thrill and confuse me, teach me pride and anger, or make me happy and sad. I can not help myself. I can get completely lost in your wonderful photographs, though I'm not so sure how you mean them now. Science is precise. If the spectral fingerprint of a supernova is the same as the fingerprint of the molecule I have been studying, the meaning is clear. They are on the same chemical hand.

Sometimes you remind me of the man who in 1928 attempted to patent 'negative feedback'. He failed, just as you will. You will see the positive side of us yet. When you rebuild cameras you revise the history of seeing. I have already asked you to find our past for us, if it is to be found, if it exists at all anymore. You know what to look for, better than we do, but you do not understand that yet. For us, the war is still alive too. The world before may never be again. 'Where did it go?' my father always asks. My *Chef* asks also, but not publicly. He does not dare, as long as foreign troops still occupy his land.

In your first picture of me, I was reborn one hundred years ago, I thought, but was I? Somehow I too feel ruined still, even though I know that is not true anymore. You have given me new life. Normally love is tense, desperate, a nightmare, or it is dull, tedious and restrictive. But you are not like anyone else. We must find a way. Perhaps our differences will disappear in the baby. Between my blue eyes and your darkness, my science and your strangeness, we must come together, inevitably, as one, in our child. The best chemist in the world is the living human cell. But I won't forget my molecules with a baby around, regardless. Titles, like my doctorate, are very important here. They appear on your passport. And the law entitles our child to an education equal to mine. We must provide it.

My mother instructs me, to bring up our unborn baby as

she raised me: feed it by the scale, spank it to sleep, change its diaper only when it cries, don't let it eat on its own, put it outside when it weeps. If I had known how she nourished me, I would never have been her daughter. I grew up afraid of everything, even the stars, but thinking myself better than everybody. In fact I was till I went to study in the U.S., hoping to conquer it along with my fears. But I became stupid there, by comparison. I exaggerate, but not overly. My mother does not relent. She jabbers constantly at me, even when I am phoning you. "Research!" she says, "Research you must do here. Forget André. I will take care of the baby. It will be my present to myself."

I know, the more I complain about my mother the more I act like her. But I am to be the mother now, and I must be different. You equally must avoid my father. Please do not get the wrong impression. He is my father, whether I want him to be or not, just as you are my master now, even if I never admit it again. Sometimes I think I do not deserve so much happiness. I remember what you said in bed one night: 'If I can't give you sight, I can give you life.'

It is true. But would you now take it away? My father told me, that you have begun working for him. Are you aware that you are? He will lead you into trouble if you let him.

Nonetheless, he thanks you too, for offering us your table set from Silesia. In part our family history was lost when our dinnerware was destroyed. I believe my father when he says this. He swore to me also, that the photographic plates he gave you portray German victims of Russian revenge. He may or may not be telling the truth, but he wanted you to sell the pictures to the German press, who is paying ever so well for such things right now. Your words would be believed, but then you would be a traitor among Russians, one of us really, but beneath our contempt. This is unfair.

I must tell you though, that I have seen your letters to Nili.
I like to read your mail, even when it is not to me. Now you
know.

You wrote to her, that my country was married to yours,
that we want our lives back now. Yes, Yes, we want a divorce.
But do you know, that ridicule also rules my father's smile
for you? His snicker is a sneer. His ease with you is to weaken
your defenses. I am sorry, but his sarcasm is adjusted to deceive
you. He can not help himself. He climbs, he dives, but life on
the level is not for him. I trust you will do what you have to
once more.

I am concerned with my mother and you with my father,
or rather my father is distressed by you, and my mother by me.
They too will do what they must. Be careful.

I hate politics really. I like science because it is black and
white and irrefutable. Even though science is of its time, it is
the one cultural product that can be measured, tested and
taught precisely. It has repeatability.

I miss my experiments. One day at last I will discover the
next new element, and name it after a feminist, myself perhaps,
as I have suffered for being a woman, more than you can know.

In trying to escape my present half-life, I must remain
in Vienna a while longer, to contain and deactivate my mother
somehow. Her energies reach around the world after me. Please
bear with me, even if my efforts are futile.

love, Sara

Dear Sara,

As you wish. Meanwhile, your father informs me, that he's
donating my dishes as his own, to the First Austrian Silesian
Museum, in Vienna. The Museum exhibits artifacts from
Silesia during the time it was Austrian, before Germany took it
away and Poland captured it back. The plates were only studio
props to me, but they're pottles of pride to your father. He
already has other craft items in the Museum of the Tobacco
Monopoly and with the Treasury of the German Order, also
in Vienna. So he says.

You're right. He's quite devious, your old man, if he thinks
that I'm working for him. However, if destabilizing Germany
is in Austria's interest also, then we do share a common goal.

But you're spying on me too, while showing the way.
Thanks for warning me. I'll be wary. I didn't know that U.S.
Government communiques could be unscrambled so easily.
I might've confessed to crimes I haven't committed yet.

Your laser books have inspired me with possibilities.
I'm not about to compete with you, but I can imagine a
photograph made from microlasers, each quantum well the
equivalent of a silver grain, for 3-dimensional intensity. But
gold-doping a micro-layering of molecules and attaching
electrodes to make it live is far beyond me, so I'm targeting
simpler sights for the moment, with infra-red lensing triggers.
Star-charts practice-burn so easily. I'll be paid for my accuracy.

I wish I knew what secrets and dangers are locked away in
your lab cabinets. I hope the baby is genetically indifferent to
his mother's mind-bombs.

By the way, I went back to Kassel, to the *Alles für das Kind* store. A tank roared past, so loudly I flinched. A car with a flower bouquet on its hood followed closely. Given the somber silence within, I couldn't tell if a wedding or funeral was happening.

Life! I bought a baby bed, regardless. And a flannel sheet to love you on.

I've also been enjoying my real heritage. Not the painted plates, but pictures of the marshes and the steppes of Russia. Pictures I found in government archives here, in preparation for World War One. The vast emptiness, the wet ambiguous ground, the sweltering sunsets, the lonely mud, the steaming ice, the torn coat of a peasant a lifetime from home, things I've seen before, now made me feel more Russian than American, but I'm not that foolish to fall in love with my faults.

Take good care of yourself too.

André

Dear Sara,

It's 3 A.M. Alone and isolated, living in your apartment without you, or any word from you all week, I slip into dreams too easily. My imagination screams things I don't like hearing. Still I persevere at my work, but I've weird premonitions, a sense of horrible betrayal. Something's wrong, beyond my knowing. My photographs can't tell me what's missing. The closet darkroom only intensifies my dread. The poly-fiber paper is soft, slow and holds tones beautifully, but the imagery insists on nightmares, equally soft, slow, and holding.

I guess you knew that I would reread your letters, and my own, that you keep in the etched silver box on your dresser.

Am I imposing my hopes on you also? Impossibly? I didn't realize, my dreams were so unlike yours. Are you really the special woman I wrote to, who I fell in love with? Where is she? Are my letters to someone else? Does she exist at all? Could I find her, in a woman here, in myself, in someone I've left behind? Is she actually who I've been searching for, traveling far and wide?

Am I indeed like your DDR, awakening too late to my self-deception, from my dream of a millennial unity and Polynesian neckties? You must think the same. "You're so real!" you say, in surprise, every time I return. What dream is it that we share? Is it still hidden from us, as unformed as the baby? Your long face is pulled up by your smile so rarely now. The stark reality of you, versus the romance of my words, often surprises me but I still write to you, in fact and in my mind. Till now I haven't questioned your being or my dream, only the details of each day and the webs they shape.

Maybe you see your dreams differently, or understand the deeper need for them, and that's enough. Or are you as simple as you say you are sometimes? Impossible! Definitely. How can

a scientist, buried in her sub-routines, living in logic gates, with
ratio mirrors and thermal runways, calculating her choices
between the genetic abnormalities of one truth table over
another, be so lost? Even in love you vacillate between romantic
calm and cynical desperation. Ambivalence just gives me the
butterflies.

Am I wrong? It's as if I've been seeing you for the first time,
through an anamorphic lens, that cartoons you smaller
in one dimension, but, rotated, stretches you into epic propor-
tions. The lens gives you a morphism that you don't really have.
Similarly, when I see you through your smile, you're radiance
blinds me to your negative side.

Perhaps pregnant women are another breed. The only
time I've felt a sense of community here was on the beach this
summer. The men seemed to assume a common wife, in every
woman. Or was I the only one? Then again, I see you always
undressed, no matter what you're wearing. Other women look
so different with their clothes on. But you can separate yourself
from me so easily. Equally, I admit, sometimes I think I'm in
love with someone else, every woman but you, but that's not
true, only when anger starves my eyes.

I used to be jealous of your colleagues but after seeing
a photo of you on your mother's lap, I realize, she is who
you think you're being unfaithful to. In her severity, she
dominates your photo album, with her white face and yellow
eyes, like death-over-easy. Sorry. As you read my mail, so I'm
looking into your nooks and corners.

I had to. You've changed so much, in your sensibilities, as
well as to me. When I arrived, your were leading the normal
post-student life, with political groupies and correct human
mice, but every glint of light worried you, as though a laser
beam were loose. You were always coffeed up, and rubbing
your face, and losing everything. I wondered then, how I

could've been so blind, I'd never seen you like this. Your thinness and unease disturbed me. That you didn't recognize how fragile you'd become distressed me more. Sensing your need for me, I could only fill it. But you sneered at my way of caring. Several times I dreamt, the more you laughed inwardly, the more your features withdrew from your face, leaving your skin hanging, empty, your nose disappearing, your eyes wells in a wrinkled landscape. Pregnant though, you changed your habits. With real life in you, you became healthy and calm again, but chased me farther away. Depleted, I awoke from my dreams definitely, like the DDR, to the nightmare of Germany, to you in its grip, to Central Europe's fatal force.

But dreams renew themselves, perversely.

Grossly overexposed, on film, the sun solarizes, reproduces itself as a small black circle in the sky, reversed in its light — like you — so I worship and defy you at once.

Normally I like my dreams. My reality is a dream of you still. At night, when we're together, holding your belly is holding the baby. Sometimes suddenly I realize, there are 3 of us in bed, and the third is the unknown shape of the future.

Till now, my cameras were my children. Buying one, I adopted it, and cared for it similarly. After all, it must be fed oil, exercised, dusted and cleaned regularly.

The darkroom at your lab was unused for a long time. My hand crumbled the metal lid of the hypo jar, into rusty flaked ashes. Poor laboratory parents you guys are!

I guess, it's not the cultural web in itself that's the problem. It's as much the world I've lived in alone, back home, on the California coast, off-road in New Mexico, in the red rock of box canyons, that seeds the difference. Watching, just watching.

I remember, you looking at the northern lights and seeing 3 million volts. Everywhere you find electromagnetic fields, even in the view out the window. You don't know the difference

between a leopard and a tiger, or a goose and a turkey, or a
dustball and a spider egg. They have different energies, cooked
and raw, you said. You call greenery a waste of city space, but
you're very familiar with the boiled roots of local menus.

And so here I am in my isolation, trapped in your tiny
apartment, in this mini-concentration camp, with a TV that
only speaks German. And so I'm making ultra-high-powered
scopes to see my way out of here.

My dreams get stranger and stranger. The daily challenge of
you exhausts me, even when you're not here. Nightmares chase
me through the dark.

A baby, like a wet new-born bird, falling from its nest, slips
through my hands, into loose damp beach sand and suffocates.

A strap-shirted man with 30" mountain-peak biceps
invites me to arm-wrestle. A crippled 6-year-old boy, his
bones lumping his thin skin, watches. His flashing dark eyes
emphasize his oversized head, as he continues to wither.

Hiding, Nili cautions me, from under an aluminized space
blanket, "Helium light burning on the horizon!" she whispers.

Clowns breathe fire at a circus audience. No one complains.
Russians aren't subject to the law here. The blue-red electric
blast of air explodes three rows of eyes.

Synthesizer echoes, like babies crying in a coffee shop,
subdue the unborn. The cherry-pit people program fetal cell
death for everyone.

A dark-suited decoy, with his third vertebrae circled in
infra-red, falls down dead. A shot, like a scream of release,
shock-waves the air. The mayor's glass case shatters.

Those were last night's dreams.

Awake I know, I'm close to the edge. I am going crazy.
Definitely! I must get out of here for awhile, go rummage in my
own roots again, eat of them, enjoy them, even if I only achieve
a stomach ache and different hallucinations.

Conversely, you should avoid your mother's pot, as well as

her person. The more you complain about her, that's right, the more you act like her. When you simmer in irritation, resenting the crumbs, the smells, the spills, the dust of living, you are your mother.

Obviously, I'm afraid, for you, for me, for the baby. And the sonogram isn't convincing my unconscious.

Tonight I had the worst dream of all. I woke up with my heart pounding, but it didn't trip over itself, so I survived, but my ears rung for almost an hour, I dreamt that you and I were two halves of a checkerboard torn apart and falling. The red and black squares of my side were beating in opposite directions, trying to tear loose from each other.

This isn't the time to send you this letter, I'm sure, not while you're still pregnant. Perhaps not ever. But at least I've exhausted the anger on my tongue and the confusion in my eyes, and can save my confession in your computer. I'd rather. Your matrix printer sounds like a riveter at work now.

In any case, the darkroom is done, including the final selenium toning, though I feel as if I've been living in a uranium nitrate bath, while making the show prints. Uranium adds invisible density to a negative, yet the intensification is of limited permanence. Hopefully the decay rate of this experience is less than my lifetime. Besides which, the subtleties of selenium are preferable and that process is poisonous enough. I need an 11x14 lens, like a porthole, out of here!

Damn! I just sneezed six sheets of paper off the desk.

Our dreams are undeniable.

love,
André

Dear André,

I am certain now, and assured. I can assure you. After the baby
is born I will return to the U.S., if my application is accepted.
But I must know, will my liaison with you help or hurt, for
government work? I sense the damage my father may do, but
he told me worse news about you, that you are meeting with
the Red Army Faction, to sell them your infra-red night scopes.
Is this true? I hope not. You will be caught, or fail, or both.
You are as unsophisticated in opto-electronics as in computers.
To me, the metallic screech of my printer sounds of music, like
someone zipping up a robot. Yes, yes, I can read your entries
from here, even after you have erased them. My creation serves
me. Its logic is mine. You should have sent your last letter.
Pregnancy protects me. I am not as vulnerable as previously.
Besides you love me even if it is to spite yourself. I too am
having strange dreams, and your idea about gold-doping
quantum wells for living images is a good one. I can develop it.
My father is privy to many possibilities, thanks of his former
political status. Your federal government once asked for his
help, to borrow our cultural icons and artifacts, so that your
CIA could make holographic copies for us, in case the originals
were ever destroyed in a future war. A sporting idea, I must say.
But a sculptured laser screen would be more impressive. I have
submitted a funding proposal to research and produce one, in
the U.S. It could lead to true three-dimensional television
wafers. But not if you undermine me, not if you follow my
father's leading.

Ja, Ja, my father believes every foreigner is working for
him, knowingly or not. As he says, it is nice to have slaves but
why can't they live in their own country?

I'm trying to get my mother to go with me, at least as far as
France, for a vacation from herself. 'The French, *pshaw,* who
needs them?' she said. She says the same about all men. She is

her own answer. You and my father may as well be dead.

I am beginning to believe, as you, that my mother poisoned me deliberately, to keep me here with the baby, to take care of her. She has forced me to choose between you and her. If I stay, I will have no choice but to become like her. The thought is intolerable. I must leave. From now on, you will be my master or I must be yours. I can learn no other way. *Ja Ja*, to be in love is to be born again. I will be reborn with the baby, for certain. Your *Frau Doktor* will turn into a milk factory. That is bad enough. I will not have the baby born in Freud's waiting room also. The baby is a barrier to my life here, in any case. I would not be accepted without you, or with you now, but you accept me, I know it. The baby after all is yours and needs and will want a father. Yes, yes, I love you. You are the father of my child. As you have your hesitations, I still have mine. In the beginning I lacked perspective, had unreal expectations, my desperation was awful. The situation itself caused the romance. But I have grown, inside and out.

Coming here, I crossed a border in myself, that can not be recrossed, even if I never go anywhere again. I belong else-where, with you. I will never again be alone.

My mother was always my best excuse. Yet, except for the guilt she made me feel, I thought I could leave her behind. I could not till now. She is healed, in a way that I will never be. Her beliefs make her whole. Mine fragment me.

But I do not want to go back to the present lab environ-ment either. I do not have enough energy to do science and fight the maleness here, at the same time. When I do not work, no one gets very upset, but when my laser is out, everyone scurries around in a panic. Still the baby must be born some-where. Yes, yes, daily the monster in me grows, like a marsh-mallow in the microwave.

Sara

"André, I'm having trouble filling out the I.N.S. forms."

"Why? You've a lifetime visa."

"It is your fault. Everything is your fault. I will never forgive you. If you were not so impossible, I would have married you long ago."

"Why're you yelling at me!"

"I yell as I please. Why must we go to the U.S. anyway?"

"That's where I live."

"The toilet paper is too soft."

"Your father can recycle his for you."

"What is that supposed to mean?"

"Maybe I was referring to your claim that Hitler, for lack of paper proof, was an innocent. No hard copy exists of his orders for concentration camps, for example."

"I said that?"

"You said that."

"I know what my excuse is. I had to be very mad at you."

"You're always mad at me."

"With good reason. The baby will need a visa too. I will have to lie about you again. To admit that the baby's father is American means certain denial. The consulate will think I am tracking you or after welfare payments or hungry. No government protects an alien bastard —"

"Stop it!"

"No! Why am I having this child? Nili burst into tears at the news of my pregnancy. I hear that her husband bought her a baroque pearl much like a milky molar, to console her. I told her, 'Do not worry. Anyone can get pregnant.' It is true, is it not?"

"Sara! Why're you so jealous of Nili? She pushed me at you.
She inspired me in your direction. You've more in common
than you think."

"You?"

"No. I mean, you both are expert with numbers, for
instance, but you would master them. She regards them
as her muse."

"Do not say anymore. You will regret it."

"I already do."

"I still will not marry you."

"Okay, but why?

"You were right about my mother."

"Impossible."

"No, it is true. I always thought, no one really could love
me but Mama. You put up with me at my worst. I say what
I want to you. You must love me, as much as she ever has."

"So we don't have to convert?"

"To our best selves, yes, we must. I can not be Jewish. They
do not forgive Germany. Word War Two was the third time in
history that Germany tried to annihilate them. The Rothschild
Museum shows this. In the U.S., three strikes and you are out,
yes? You see, I am learning. We must become who we want to
be, children of science and the natural, free of a country. Please,
you will teach me."

"If you give me a chance — By the way, the Holocaust
Museum said, your father was misinformed. The victims in
the glass plates seem to be Polish soldiers prior to 1900."

"Oh."

"Maybe your great-grandfather was involved, the one in
the military band?"

"Enough. I am coming back, but you will get no kisses
from me tonight."

Dear Nili,

Regular post is the surest form of privacy these days. Sara can access anything electronically. I have to assume she's not the only one, regardless of scramblers, shredders, laws, etc. But her parents send her cash in the mail regularly. It always arrives safely.

It seems now, we'll be returning to San Francisco after all. Sara's receiving recognition for her graduate research in the U.S., for discovering cobalt in a second supernova. But she's more excited about the possibilities of a next form of image-making, in which the laser surface itself is the photograph, through which her history can reveal itself, etched forever in space. A grant is pending.

She's quiet about my cameras now. Still, a lens-box from the 1890s is like a lost family crest to her. My collection clutters her living room, and satisfies her immensely, I can tell, regardless of what she says.

But I'm writing for another reason, to ask for my store front back, in exchange for which your husband can handle the business end, of Sara's visionary science, when and if it comes into actual sight.

I'd rather settle in up the coast, with space to spread out, but Sara has no interest in nature really. She enjoys the heated closeness and crowded conditions of the lab, the sense of security that locked doors grant. When she grew up, an open window brought hostile exposure if not freezing conditions.

As pregnant as she is, she still persists at the lab. I sit all day in the apartment and fret, fret, fret. Nevertheless, we'll need a protected laboratory environment in San Francisco, with maximum power provisions, as well as a place to live with the baby, however he's shaped. My shop doesn't qualify, but Sara and I began there.

The phone's ringing.

Sara's in labor!

My anxiety apart, Sara never worried. She refused to the end all thorough testing. The doctor was sure she'd need a Cesarean, with her narrow hips. The magic voice of the midwife made all the difference though. And I held onto Sara the entire time. Labor was brief, five hours. The baby pushed out, crying loudly, perfectly fine, dark like myself. Strong and alert. A nine pound boy! Sara was shocked. "It never occurred to me, that I would have a male child," she said in despair. The delivery itself was less difficult, the pain intense but brief, an instamatic birth in effect. No thought, no focusing needed. Nature did take care of everything. Though Sara needed a few stitches. I cut the umbilical cord. And the placenta went to a cosmetics company. We're having the baby circumcised, as if he were in the U.S., but formally we're still unbelievers. Nature is more magnificent than we can conceive. Indeed a new born covered with cheese and blood beggars all belief. Definitely.

I feel drained, happy, relieved. That the baby's whole and normal means something. So far the baby is without a name. I keep suggesting Smoke, Shadow, Super and such. Sara wants to call him by the name of a new metal, that she hasn't discovered yet. By law here the name must indicate the baby's sex, i.e., there's a recommended list. Deviations need to be court approved.

City hall handed us an 8-page form to fill out, requesting my grandmother's birth certificate, as well as detailed financial statements from me. If we had benefits coming, okay, but as aliens we're nowhere. Sara filled in her part willingly. I refused. The clerk did his cum-un-zee-here number. I told him that I didn't recognize his authority over me. He shrugged and said to Sara, "A reluctant father, yes?" Sara said no. In the end, as I did not fit into the cubbyhole culture of the bureaucrat, he tore up my forms. "This is none of Germany's business. You both are foreigners," he said dismissingly. "You're the fucking alien!" I answered.

Outside I realized that I meant it. It's the Russian in me, and the American, and the voices I hear. When pushed, my beliefs instantly surface. Deep inside I don't accept the government here or its right to the land. Germans are trespassers on my earth. In fact they feel very dispossessed in the presence of foreigners, especially disobedient ones. My father would approve.

Sara keeps saying, I better watch myself. But I'm not here to be cautious. Sara remind me that there are good Germans also. I hear her but I don't listen. I unbolted my license plate, put it back on upside down, and added a decal of the imperial eagle in skeletal form to my windshield. At the same time I'm collecting U.S. stamps with German postmarks, after-canceled as it were, because the U.S. missed. Yup, clerks here postmark the unmarked stamps coming into the country, so they can't be used again at home. Many well-wishers sent congratulations, to my surprise.

That the baby's a boy still troubles Sara, but she'll get used to it, I hope. He's nursing nicely. With Halloween near though, it's as if he's already chased by ghosts from the graveyard. Every so often he gives out a loud inexplicable wail that subsides into tense twisted cries. Invariably the wind blows his blanket off, whenever I take him outside.

I know when you suggested, "Have a child with Sara," you expected something boring and folksy. But it seems Sara and I will always behave badly.

I guess everyone thinks so. A telegram came today from the embassy requesting that I call for an immediate interview, and prepare to return to the U.S. as soon as possible. Is my passport being pulled?

Does the squid have eight heads? Do they talk to each other? I can't believe that they do. Why else the conflicting messages? I was asked to pinpoint economic targets. Don't these include the human kind? I was asked to respect our government's advantage, to report, to connect, to hand-deliver letters, to encourage a U.S. point of view. And I've done so, not always politely, I admit, but I've broken no laws yet. Or I've been excused from them by the local enforcers. Have I suddenly become an embarrassment, in diplomatic terms? Does State think I'll kill someone myself, without Agency approval? Who's complaining about me?

I won't leave here till I'm ready, and if I'm forced out I'll make the event a spectacle, I promise.

Please inform me as to what's going on — unless I'm meant to operate on my own conclusions.

You should know, Svedlini, your Russian, sent me something I don't have, a ",*Спорт*'", a Sport, the world's first 35mm SLR, made in 1935 in Leningrad, and asked me to photograph you, for him, as part of a world he may never know.

Yours, as always,
André

"André, are you all right? Did the interview go well?"

"Sorry, Sara, I was too proud of my work. I bragged. I've been uncovered, and recalled. As of today my passport's invalid, for associating with terrorists. I made and sold illegal, ultra-high-powered scopes, with a range of 1,000 yards."

"Did you silhouette targets on the sights?"

"I etched spinal columns on the cross-hairs."

"Using my laser? Without my help? How could you?"

"Easily. But you'll like this less. The terrorist, I'm suspected of plotting with, is your father."

"What? How could that be? It is stretching the meaning of terrorism."

"Germany doesn't think so, or the U.S. Your father wants Germany's southern provinces returned to Austria. He gave a speech comparing the destabilization in Yugoslavia to the potential benefits of upheaval in Germany."

"He is a fool. What are you going to do?"

"Nothing. The consulate asked me to avoid him."

"But he is coming next week, to see the baby."

"Then I'll have to leave before then."

"No. Go to Köln, have your show, the one my father and the Institute helped you arrange. You have the right."

"I was hoping to take you, with our son, to see it."

"We will attend an opening in the U.S. —"

"— if the Goethe Institute doesn't reverse itself."

"My father was right. You are politically naive, like most Americans. Our son will learn better."

"Definitely. I'm going to teach him."

"Since you did not ask, I will tell you. I instruct him."

"Will we ever agree?"

"There will be peace, when you also surrender!"

Dear Son,

Even if I'm not on your birth certificate, I'm your father, what-ever wrong I've done in the name of right. You can invoke me for good or bad as you need. You've also a claim, a head start at least, toward U.S. citizenship in the future. You'll need it. Europe is the land of looking behind you.

My camera collection and tools are yours too. If I'm unable to teach you their use, ask your mother to try. As a Doctor of Astro-Chemistry, she doesn't know her earthly limits however. She sees a blip on a screen as 100 billion suns 100 billion light years away. Strangely she's probably right. But her lab needs larger and larger unaffordable machines to see smaller and smaller invisible things. Yet her extra-territorial mind is immense indeed. If in the dust of a stellar nursery, a star is born, she understands the process. She's too educated about too little, though. I hope you roam the more natural path, and follow the flood plain, into the human sea. My cameras may guide you.

I'm off now, to meet my fate. Also your mother doesn't like my "imperialism" in her kitchen. I tell her what to eat to feed you.

Your mother and I are very different. Sometimes we can't communicate, at any wave-length, from radio to X-ray, as she says. Nevertheless you're our bond, forever.

You're also the eyes of the future, as well as the vision ahead. Perhaps one day you'll see our dreams and be able to take their reality for granted. I hope you'll learn U.S. ways. Life isn't layered, cultures are. Sure, we're a billion micro-lasers, projecting our beliefs at each other. But we're still more. Definitely!

Your mother and I met during a transitional time, in a

beautiful city. But San Francisco paved over the changes that its earthquake promised.

Enjoy every freedom you're given, break the mold wherever you go, turn the soil and plow to grow, improvise on your findings, and treat the world as a rare and special plant. You'll do brilliantly. Your mommy will teach you whatever else you should know. But your maternal grandfather needs to be forgotten, left to mummify in the museums.

My father was a hero to me. My mother, your grandmother, died when I was ten, and I never got to know her beyond her care for me. Few letters or pictures were left behind. Her face floats through my thoughts regularly. She is a shadow in my head. Your mother is the substance. They look strangely alike, though I'm not sure I can define the similarity, because it ends there. It is only skin deep. But my mother would have loved you very much, as your mother will one day. No matter what, I remain

Your loving father,
André Optic

Dear Sara,

Back on the road. The pen-point highway signs detoured me
around Cologne, but I found my exhibit in one of 150 booths
in the second of 5 halls at the Photokina. The event is garish,
inflated, too much for one day, but fun nonetheless. Olympus
used rap-robot imitators as shills. Polaroid built a wall with 120
cameras in synch, to produce life-sized image-collages. Leica
set up a grandstand with a unique camera for each seat. Nikon
let me play with its latest baby, a 6-lb 6-mm 2.8 lens that sees
220 degrees. Kodak and everyone else took a quality step backward with family album c.d's. Lagerfeld introduced PHOTO, a
scent for men. Yes, "a man, a woman, a camera." It's already in
the stores, bottled like a grenade. Should I try it? Basically there
was nothing altogether new, no technological leaps of excel-
lence toward a new era, only extensions and refinements of the
current presence.

The same is true of my exhibit, but this serves the point.
I wrote a brief statement of intent to hang with the prints. The
magazine sponsoring the space for my show opposed me, till I
convinced the publisher of what he already knew — sarcasm
sells well amidst smugness. Let me know what you think. After
all it's dedicated to you, my dear:

To witness Reunification, I brought a 1936 Leica,
loaded with T-Max 3200 and shot from the hip,
American style, unobtrusively, quietly, in motion.
By developing the film with infinite care (soaking it
overnight in a refrigerator), and thus keeping grain to
a minimum, I rendered in full-tones the blindering
cold.

Like it? I didn't think so. Yup, my blunt irony is negative,
but not the technical achievement. The passing audience
appreciated the stark naturalness I pulled from the dark.

Returning, wishing you with me, I triangled to Frankfurt
for the Book Fair, hoping to find a helpful American or two.
I didn't. You didn't miss anything at the fair either, except order
forms, sales anxiety, over-load and confusion. The intense
quiet of the books themselves seemed lost. A beautiful volume
on the mountains of Tibet only briefly transported me out

of the maze. One San Francisco publisher, who I'd met before, was forced to borrow money from his editor to pay for the "furniture" of the booth. Needless to say, I didn't ask him about printing my photographs in book form. He would've jumped through a hoop for a Red Cross hot-dog. There were none.

Tomorrow I'll head for Bonn, to the embassy. Hopefully I'll be home before this letter. It's come a long way. Perhaps I've gone too far myself. Sometimes I feel like a broken tile, who's fallen off the wall of his life. The felt need to build a new house, starting from scratch, drives me to consider abandoning everything and returning to be what I was brought up to be, whatever that is. But I feel so far away from it, that the picture isn't clear enough for a plan.

The photographs that I make now, with my cameras, are substitute tiles of a sort. They fit together cleanly, like prefabricated blocks that I've poured. They rebuild the landscape with a crystalline clarity and contain it, and keep me from running away.

Here's a copy of the handout, reproducing some of the prints from my show. Sorry. The picture of you wasn't used.

Love,
André

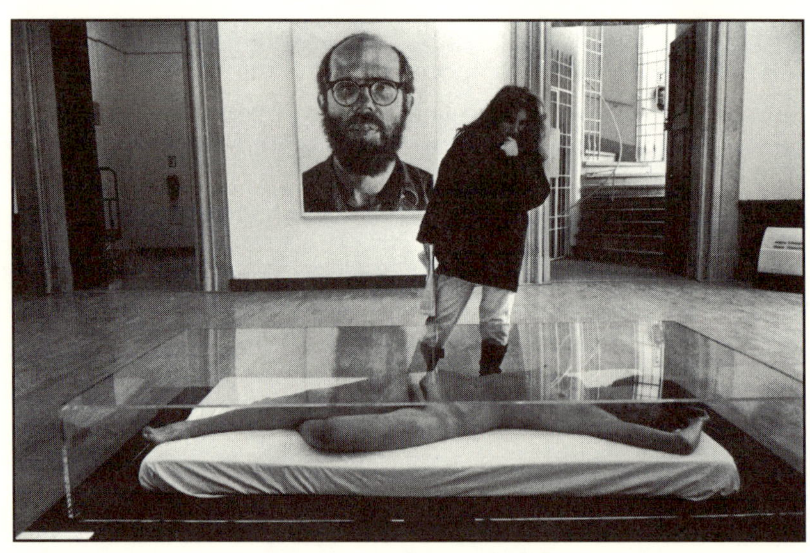

POLIZEI
CONNY IS
WIR

Dear André,

Congratulations! I like your pictures. Surprised?

Mail to Bonn is quick, so this will be waiting for you. I wish you were here instead of my father. He did not come to see our baby. He is here to compete with him, to be the baby himself. He expects me to spoil him, as if he were a child, in ways that I was never indulged. He shouts angrily for attention whenever our son cries. Because I ignore the man, he treats himself like an infant, without restraint, satisfying every oral craving. He came to me to hide from his nurse-wife. Yes, he did. The food she disallows, in the interest of health, he gorges on here. Each day he cooks bacon with butter, and eggs in butter, and drinks two bottles of sweet licorice wine.

He is not as competitive with you for my attention. You have served his purpose it seems, in your own perverse way. I think, that you inspire his rudeness. He trusts your perversity. He sees it as his opportunity. He is unaware that you are not just churlish. You do nothing simply. You are more demanding than crystals in your search for clarity. My father does not look elsewhere, to escape his nurse-wife. He is here to tell me what to do. He is ill-mannered to upset me. He says that I should curtsy to him like my mother used to. She never did. I do not know what he is thinking. He is rewriting his past. He has joined openly with the right-wing party. He knows that it will destroy my chances in the U.S. Maybe that is what he wants to do. I must straighten out with him or insist that he leave. It is difficult. He does not grow up, only old.

And what are you doing to help? You should be here kissing my belly back into place. I love you.

Sara

"Hi Sara, it seems the show was my moment in the sun. Now an ugly spotlight is on me. Bonn was bad news. I'm restricted to the airport. The German police exploded. They want me gone. They said, in these changing times the politicians perform their duty under mortal danger without my provocations. A siege mentality already exists. I can't say that I was only tinkering with the timetable. My embassy isn't defending me. If it has to, it'll compromise me, to save face."

"You are a fish out of water here."

"I can set up house in the U.S. before you arrive."

"Will you come back to me first?"

"I would, but the harder I step on the gas the slower the car goes. It'd make a good shipping crate though."

"The car is not allowed to leave, unless it passes inspection."

"Sell it in the East then. I can't help you with it. I have to go. Being a father is changing me. I'll leave my heart behind."

"You will take mine with you."

"Will you be all right with the baby?"

"Yes, yes, I am finished at the lab. The *Chef* is giving me three months extra pay as a present, but he expects me to formulate his next paper."

"On the new data from Russia?"

"Yes. Svedlini wrote to me to say, 'I wish you a merry motherhood.' After a list of chemical suggestions, he closed 'with all possible pious wishes.'"

"He's from another world."

"So am I."

"I won't be with you for New Year's."

"You can call. I will be home with the baby, crying and reading my feminism, alone. My father has gone."

I send you this letter to take with you, to remind you of your purpose. Whatever you first intended, our lives are one now.

Do you understand that if you succeed on the ground, I will succeed in the sky? I hope so. Our missions are intertwined. Perhaps they are also one and the same.

As you can not climb out of your gravity, I may never escape my history. I believe still, my future is to be found in the past and its bridge to space, to the stars beyond time and light, that give us the power of earth. My father would rule, but no one is favored. Even Einstein is dead, forever.

You are right to think that my views here result from a lack of sky. Indeed I long to leave because there is no space program or advanced astronomy.

I am also unsure in my beliefs, but my doubts do not erase them, just as my hesitations about you do not separate me from you anymore.

I love you and hope that our son is as loving toward me as you can be.

Yet I will always seek to climb, to conquer, yes, yes, to out-magic you, even if I do not know to what end.

We must live with ourselves.

My debts here are paid.

Please prepare a nice nest for me and our little one.

My father and mother are flowerpots. They grow weeds.

love,
Sara

It's stranger than strange, my welcome here. I've the sense, I've
been away to war, but am coming home to a battle zone. New
York has that aspect. The U.S. is different every time I return.
The country is wallowing in debt & recession while awash in
plenty. Outside Grand Central Station, a hustler, waving a
bundle of credit card applications guaranteeing "$50,000 a
year", punched a legless veteran selling pencils from a wheel-
chair. In the lobby, a born-again delta blues singer performed
ably, while in the men's room a derelict rushed past the busy
urinals to piss in a garbage can. But the flow of Brooks Brothers
suits went on uninterrupted, even when another fight exploded
in front of a bar, leaving two men face down on the granite
floor. Meanwhile, the waiting room looked like a bomb shelter
with bedraggled refugees still holding out hope 20 years later.

In the galleries, I found Cheshire cars and glass-plate ghost-
ships, and compliments for my photos, but no interest in
exhibiting their hard edged normalcy.

After a day in the city, I returned to Kennedy Airport, to
enjoy the world terminal dance. A Spanish teacher, off to
winter by herself in Greece, circled an arriving Frenchman,
here to try on some English.

Coming from Frankfurt, where military police strut
through the airport with machine guns and bomb-sniffing
dogs on short leashes, I laughed at the laxity here, then felt at
home. Security agents in Frankfurt threatened my cameras
with a compression chamber, as a test for hidden explosives,
until I emptied the film.

Back in the San Francisco Bay Area, new hippies, in silk
paisley, blond Indian braids, and a look of deep concern,
mingled with the latest in-wave-shaggy wool army sweaters
and terraced hair. At a glance, I decided our future wasn't here

either. When a hundred other tin-types joined together,
to close the bridge in angry protest marches, I knew we had to
try somewhere else. The political rain is stale in San Francisco
lately. The peninsula thumb has lost its silicon grip on the
future for the moment also. Marin is building retirement
homes for musicians. The music scene in the city is still thrash
& variation. Neo-Mesmo & Slink, as styles, never came in.
They're not even floating off-shore.

Nili could only suggest Colorado, or New Mexico, for us.
I've made the trip before, to explore that time warp, with tire-
tread clouds all day and diesels idling all night. But I did it
again. On I-40 in Arizona, I discovered 'rain for rent,' the golf-
ball-house abandoned in the sand trap desert, a wine-red river
near Main Drain Road, Miss Moo selling music and guns, and
a gleaming moon in the plateau sky.

Knowing your aversion to the labs in New Mexico, and
uncertain as to what my reception might be, I skipped ahead to
Colorado, as our best compromise. The ski-state also sells itself
as the mountains of Germany. But the sign at the Stage Stop
Inn is lettered down to St. Gestop. Interlocking shopping
centers surround the main university center. Its women live
in four-wheel drive. Municipal glaciers feed its water supply.

After New Mexico invents the bombs, the beer-drinking
Colorado turkey-eaters construct them, is how it works, demo-
graphically. So, do you want to ski in robot-dress-wear, and be
part of the desert-dry white-face? Me neither.

Returning, I met a migrating lightning storm in Wyoming,
the radioactive state. Thundering wind stopped the car. A
massive funnel came down and went back up, right in front of
me. I knew immediately, this is home. Our experimental hive
would survive unnoticed. We'd be on our own. What say,
honey bee? Your driving drone loves you still.

André

Dear André,

I have bad news. First, my grant application was denied. But I faxed an abstract of my *Chef's* last paper, of which I am second author, to a conference in Los Angeles, and I am accepted to speak. At about the same time, the American Vacuum Society is meeting in Philadelphia. I may also attend.

Another unfortunate news is that my mother had a second stroke, much worse this time. I am in Vienna with her. Though her mind is functioning, her body is not. She sleeps with her eyes open. I have to shut them for her. It is the scariest thing, to see her staring at me, without vision. I'm inclined to leave her here in the care of my father and his late-life nurse. It will serve him right. My mother will have her revenge on him yet. But not on me. I will not let her make me responsible for her collapse. She should have shared our happiness in the little one.

He is fine, sturdy. He laughs alot, and enjoys swiveling his large head like a loony bird. He cries like our car. He shuts off his tears with abrupt shuddering, then collapses. He starts up like a diesel too, wheezing faster and faster till he coughs into tears. I am discovering rhythms in me that I did not know I had, bouncing him on my knee, in syncopation.

You will like my nipples. They have grown immense, nursing. But I have bad dreams. I worry about things, like the diamond window clouding my observation of metallic hydrogen in the making. The metal is transparent, but it closes down in my nightmares. My mother has pulled the blinds.

I still want to build the imaging laser with you. During the day, while the baby sleeps, I often stare out wistfully at the snow and imagine a million unseen candles lighting spontaneously. At night the ice flowers on the glass tell me the same: however long it takes, we must succeed. We will create a new way to see, between us, and still be ourselves.

I have always hated the snow, because my parents made
me vacation with them. Skiing is boring, expensive, and a
dangerous time waste. I do not change my mind. I am glad
you rejected Colorado. Wyoming is the right place for future.
You have not failed me. And I will not fail you.

I can not wait to leave. Now is the time that people in
Vienna line the streets, holding hands and lit candles,
in religious union. Everyone must run this gauntlet of belief.
I wish you were here to spit at their hypocritical purity. I can
not. It is my tradition also, to decry those who do not worship
us blindly. My mother is dead for all practical purposes.
I should be free. I would be, but I am unsure of myself. My
father asks me though, whether I am enjoying my freedom
as a woman. He is referring to the liberty you allow me. He
would never be so kind.

I saw on TV the protests in San Francisco versus the
cheering in New York, for war with Iraq. Before my departure,
there was much protesting in Germany also, by the anti-war-
riors. Mostly they stood around looking lost, spoiling for a
fight. It was as if they were stranded in the long-term parking
lot without an arena pass. They do not want to know that
Germany has been left out of the war. The army does know
and is distressed. Odo is a soldier now. He was furious when
he found out, that the Allies will not have Germany on their
side. He is rightly afraid that he will be sent to the sidelines,
to protect the Turks, the janitors of Germany, as you called
them. Of course, national television does not mention the
4 to 6 billion Mark promised by the head cabbage to fund
the Allies fight. My father knew nonetheless.

Sadly, my cousin Frowin was stabbed at a New Year's Eve
party. There are fascist and anti-fascist parties, as you know,
different faces of the same scene, reverse sides of one coin, both
wanting to win the toss, by any means, as you have said. Frowin

will live, but poorly. Send him your best wishes. You must. You owe him that. You inspired him. Yes, yes, you are his *Führer still,* in spite of his wounds, and he would martyr you to bring his abstract beliefs back to earth, so be careful. Do not let yourself be blinded. Your philosophy too is in your eyes.

I advertised, and a Russian officer came in a taxi to buy the Mercedes, but after a quick look at it, he growled, *"Nyet,* I want something better!" Svedlini meantime writes from Leningrad, to say he hopes we can visit when the time is less embarrassing for his country.

Wherever the world is going, we go together now. But it will not be Wyoming. It is not the right place yet. I am a city person first, and you will earn less of a living in the desert than in San Francisco. Till I have new grants, we must strive in ways that we know. But I will show you something, new for me. I went back to the Berlin wall, one last time. Here it is, a section still standing. At last I worked your camera. Did I not?.

Your love,
Sara

"André, I'm afraid. Come to Austria instead."

"You already have your ticket, don't you?"

"I will be an alien again, a yuppie Frau with a six-sided salami and yogurt bread. Come here."

"Damn, woman, no. The plan's made."

"Engraved in silver? Chiseled in stone?"

"Whatever. I can't stand this. Left alone, you always choose the wrong dream."

"Szo Szo."

"Enough sarcasm. All right, okay. The Society of Solar Optimists requests your presence."

"S-O-S-O. Zuper! But what lab will I have? I failed in Germany to produce a new stable metal. My results were fragmentary, because I lacked support. It is possible, at above two hundred atomic number, atoms become stable again, without radioactive decay, This could happen in the natural environment of a uranium mine. That is why Wyoming is so appealing. We will go when I have a mine of my own."

"Oh hell! Why?"

"When atoms bombard one another, sometimes they stick, it only takes one, like a sperm to an egg, like you and I, to produce a new life form, not yet known. Besides, if I do not create a new metal, our baby will never have a name."

"Won't your lasers do the job?"

"With proper controls, and if barrier energy is overcome, perhaps. The price is high but the gain is higher. Yes, it is easy, as easy goes, theoretically. No one has done it."

"What about — "

"You must not worry. I will succeed, on my own as well as with you. But we will try UC Berkeley first."

"Then be on that plane! I'll be waiting at S.F.O."

Full Moon Rising

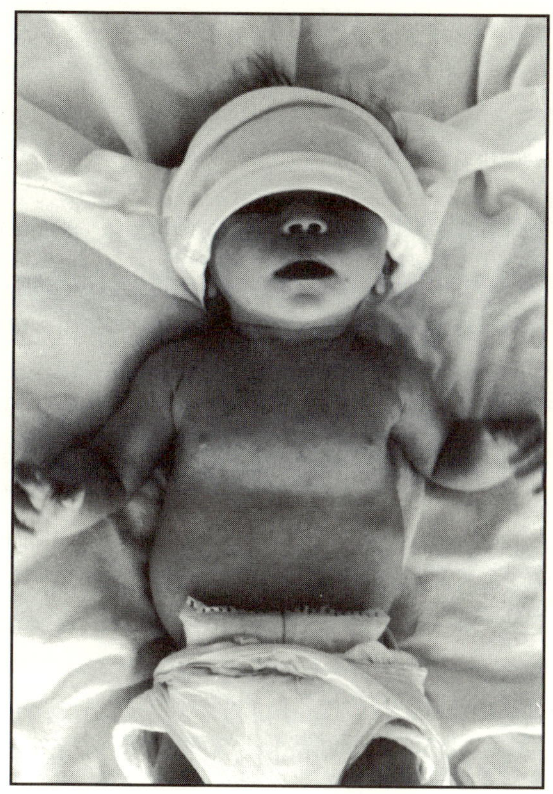

Dear Nili,

How's Washington? Thanks for your help there. I wonder what
it's like for you. You used to get the grants, now you give them
out. NASA is lucky to have you, Sara thinks. She's thankful
too for the grant you approved for her, in spite of her recent
remarks. Then again, as a scientist in love with an alien, you
are the frustrated star gazer. And as a bureaucrat in charge of
30 odd million, you are the bars on the dollar sign. That's not
bad. In fact, you've put everything in perspective for Sara.
Somehow. She seems happy. She's even becoming American
again, in spite of herself. I'm glad. My son has escaped the
numbing nursery of Vienna. Sara's father wrote to her about
Austria's plan to return some properties to the Rothschilds, for
p.r. and to humble them again. Sara can't fully escape that
mind-vise either. Her ambivalence is stunning sometimes.

Thank you also for helping me get my passport back. If I
weren't born here, I'd probably be without a country. I'm not
sure who my enemies are anymore. Though I'm free to travel
again, I haven't applied for any visas. In spite of the fire last
month, that destroyed 3,000 homes including ours in the East
Bay hills, I feel safer here. Luckily, most of our things were still
in storage. The fire didn't get them and we had time to get
everything else out of our tiny apartment. Sara thinks I caused
the fire, by just being here. Sparks follow me, you see. Actually
I'm working quietly, privately, often with your ex-husband.

Say hello to Svedlini when you talk to him again. And come
visit us in Wyoming. Thanks to your help, we're moving there
next week.

Take care,
André

11/91

Dear Friends,

We'd have sent a birth announcement before this. The baby is still unnamed. I've a list of possibles 3 pages long, so does Sara. Not one entry matches. You'd hardly know we speak the same language. Thanks to Sara's subterranean efforts in Austria, however, the baby's passport identifies him as "Brightly Berlin". André Optic isn't in the official picture.

We've been in Wyoming six months now, without scientific breakthroughs. Progress seems as slow as the baby growing. At 15 months he's beginning to speak. Sara calls him our little mouse. His first words this morning, when Sara bit into an apple, were, "Uh Oh Broken!"

Sara keeps asking at what age will he begin to obey the rules. She's filled out and healthy. I've let my hair and beard grow. Sara thinks I look like a wooly Siberian mammoth.

We live in a fracture zone, on a ledge, with a horse stable, insulated with hay bales, for my studio, not far from a uranium mine, where Sara has her lab, well funded at last, though she may require a neutron star furnace for her expectations of metals. My show still circulates but isn't a seller. And the imaging laser needs endless refinement before it's viable. We should have a name for the baby before then.

Life is quite peaceful here. Visitors are few. Watching a jack-rabbit bound through the snow, its long-eared shadow leaping across the whiteness, was entertainment enough this winter. Still cultural breakthroughs occur in small ways. At last Sara can tell a house and a barn apart. Come spring, she may score her own way in the girls fast pitch league, in Sweetwater. She wants to play, to teach her son the prowess she expects of him.

Our only real worry is the targeting scope I made last year. It's illegal, even in this country. One was used on an official who smelled too much of money, according to Norbert, Sara's ailing father. I've decided, from now on, to stick to my own family tradition, of creating forgotten inventions, that amuse and entertain only. Sara meanwhile has discovered how to clean telescope mirrors with her lasers. The dirt explodes away. CO2 snowflake sweeping is the usual means, though it's destructive to the atmosphere.

It's wonderful being this far from any political scene, or population center. There's space and time to enjoy our dreams. The world is a confusing place, and here we escape its intensity. The elements themselves shape our days. We're growing a new tyrant in our lives though. "No" and "More" are his favorite words. But he may have a brother or sister soon. We promise to name the first baby before the second. I photograph him endlessly, playing whiphand to the new moon.

Probably next month we'll wing across to the O-Reich, via Paris, to show off our little bundle of life. He'll be trilingual before long. When I say water, Sara says *Vaser*. Bird, I say. *Flugel*, says Sara. Kicken, says our little guy, and runs away giggling. Yes, he has his own language. Sara's brain-dead mother might relate to it.

Hopefully we'll drop in on Svedlini & Nili in Moscow too, and somehow visit our other relatives en route. My aunt on her throne in London, and Sara's cousins in industry, on the Danau, and her father, if we're not too embarrassing to him, now that he holds office again.

Birds filled our mailbox with a nest of grass cuttings last spring, and before we fly off, we expect to watch the chics peck their way out of their speckled blue shells.

Soon we hope we will meet again on the next crest of time.

The best to you all,
André, Sara & Brightly
5/92